A SECRET OF 1

ELLIE BLAINE 1920s MYSTERIES

A SECRET OF FEATHERS

A SECRET OF FEATHERS

*ELLIE BLAINE 1920s MYSTERIES
BOOK ONE*

EM BOLTON

ELLIE BLAINE 1920s MYSTERIES

Copyright © 2023 by EM Bolton

All rights reserved. No part of this publication may be reproduced, stored or transmitted in any form or by any means, electronic, mechanical, photocopying, recording, scanning, or otherwise without written permission from the publisher. It is illegal to copy this book, post it to a website, or distribute it by any other means without permission.

This novel is entirely a work of fiction. The names, characters and incidents portrayed in it are the work of the author's imagination. Any resemblance to actual persons, living or dead, events or localities is entirely coincidental.

EM Bolton asserts the moral right to be identified as the author of this work.
First edition
ISBN:9798870281421

For there's a change in the weather
There's a change in the sea
So from now on there'll be a change in me
Why, my walk will be be different, and my talk and my name
Nothing about me gonna be the same
I'm gonna change my way of livin', and that ain't no shock
Why, I'm thinking of changin' the way I gotta set my clock
Because nobody wants you when you're old and gray
There's gonna be some changes made today
There'll be some changes made

There'll Be Some Changes Made
Ethel Walter, 1921

ELLIE BLAINE 1920s MYSTERIES

CHAPTER 1

THIS wasn't at all how Ellie imagined England to look. She wasn't sure now what she had expected, but she was sure it wasn't this.

The rain? Yes, of course. It was the first week of April and so she would have almost been disappointed not to have a proper English shower greet her arrival. The tang of dirty saltwater and the smell of tar and coal and oil and seaweed? She'd seen the dockyards at New York and Cherbourg now and so she was sure that smell must be the same around the world.

But somehow, in her mind, England had looked just a little… happier? Brighter, maybe? Despite the clouds. Instead, the docks, the water, the sky and horizon all lay out the same dull, workday grey in every direction. The hurry of trollies and trucks and the lines of bobbing masts and funnels above endless rows of flat-topped sheds and warehouses gave the place the feel of a vast assembly line, like those her father had described when he went to see Mr Ford's factory in Michigan. Certainly it looked efficient; busier even than the port she'd left at New York, but without the same chaos and clutter or the manic, infectious energy.

It was foolish really, she thought. All she had ever seen of England was Bertie, and so maybe that's what she had expected. But of course nowhere could be that. No one could get their expectations that high and not be disappointed. And besides, she was sure any visitor from England would find Indianapolis equally as uninspiring when they first arrived there, but there was always more to a place than first impressions. She held that thought and smiled at the memory of Bertie again.

Among the flat, dull concrete and stone of Southampton docks, two buildings stood out: the faded white and red of a grand pier to one side, and the brighter white of the railway station to the other. From the clock tower of the pier she could see they had arrived right on schedule and she should be at the station in good time to meet the man who had paid for her trip.

There had been a time when she had expected to meet Bertie's family, but not like this. And anyway, that time had long passed when she finally received Dr Lindley's terse invitation, and the circumstances of their meeting were far different to those she had once had in mind.

> *Western Union Telegram*
> *London 12:03 03/11 1921*
> *Miss Eleanor Blaine*
> *Lord Melmersby dead. Family request presence at Melmersby Hall for memorial service. All travel arranged. Details to follow.*
> *Dr Richard Lindley*

The telegram had come out of the blue. She had heard from Dr Lindley only once before: that wet, cold October Friday four years previous when he broke her heart with a piece of brown paper and just enough words at a penny a letter to say his brother had died a hero's death.

And that, she thought, would be that. The Lindley family – lords of the manor, blood as blue as the background of the Union Flag – had not accepted Miss Eleanor Blaine – daughter of a race track mechanic, collar as blue as diesel smoke – when Bertie had been alive and in love with her. She certainly hadn't expected to hear from them now.

But now, it seemed, Dr Lindley – Bertie's big brother ('the serious one' he once told her) – *was* the Lindley family. The last of them. And he had invited her to England, and so here she was.

The journey over had been comfortable. A Tourist Third cabin, shared with two ladies of a certain age who found it perfectly scandalous that a young, unmarried lady should be travelling alone, and who swore to protect her from the worst kinds of men, then spent the best part of the 10-day trip matchmaking her with anyone who had a steady income and what the elder of them called 'twinkly eyes'.

She'd politely declined the further attentions of an insurance salesman from Ohio, although he had been pleasant enough company and a good match in a game of deck quoits. Then there had been the tobacco trader from Virginia. She shuddered slightly when she thought of him again, and what a waste of good Scotch whisky and soda it had been in washing any doubt about her intentions from his mind.

Those inconveniences aside, it had been a pleasant enough trip and she was pleased to discover she had what her father called 'sea legs'. But, nonetheless, as she stepped off the ship she was glad to finally be back on dry land – or at least solid ground; not much was dry now, as the morning's April shower had turned to a steady downpour.

She pulled at the handle of her trolly, cursing quietly at the one sticky wheel which did its best to take her luggage in exactly whichever direction she wasn't planning to go. A hand suddenly thrust its presence into the corner of her right eye, and she turned to see a man she had been introduced to on the boat – Derek, was it? Or David? She wasn't sure now. Either way, he was gallantly holding an umbrella above her head, allowing the heavy rain to mat his already thinning hair unflatteringly to his high forehead as he smiled at her.

"Can't let you get soaked can we? Welcome to England. I'm afraid it's like this rather a lot here. You'll get used to it."

Ellie smiled. "Thank you, um…" her hesitation just long enough that she could see a little hurt in his eyes, quickly dashed away with a hasty grin in return.

"Daniel," he said, almost apologetically, "it's Daniel. I suppose you'll be keen to see your chap after all this time? I shall expect he is fit to bursting to see you again!"

She'd found a little lack of clarity over her relationship with the man she would be meeting in England had done wonders to see off the attentions of all but the most persistent of the gentlemen her cabin mates had introduced her to.

It was usually enough to say that the son of Lord Melmersby was meeting her at the docks. It had certainly been enough to dissuade Daniel – who she now decided was a thoroughly decent gent, but that even if she had been 'one of those ladies' the two spinsters assumed travelled on ships alone, she couldn't overlook the fact he wore stacked heels and still had to stretch to get his umbrella above her head. She scolded herself for that ungenerous thought and ducked out from under the cover of the brolly which kept catching in the tight waves of her hair.

"Absolutely, he will. Thank you so much, but I think the rain is clearing now and I should probably get to the station before he finally bursts."

Daniel looked around at the rain that was still falling as heavily as ever and nodded. "Well, I shan't keep you from your lucky fellow any longer. Bon voyage and all that!"

"And to you," she said, turning the stubborn trolley sharply and dragging it and herself under the cover of an awning that ran along the side of one of the station goods sheds. Daniel waved at her as he disappeared around the corner of a redbrick cabin and Ellie smiled weakly back. She would wait here for a while, hoping for the worst of the rain to pass, then make the open walk to the foyer of the main station building, where she was to meet Dr Lindley.

He was due in on the 1:30 train from London, and it must be at least 12:30 by now, she thought. She opened the small clutch bag she took with her everywhere. It was the only 'nice thing' she had bought for herself from her salary working the sales desk of Ernie Drammer's car dealership. The rest, after keeping a house over her and her mother's head, had gone on what she considered essentials: spanners, wrenches, engine oil, kerosene – anything that could keep her father's old car going, or better yet make it go faster. Bertie had been deeply amused when he first saw the Old Pepper Pot, as her father had called it, but she'd soon wiped the smile off his face taking him round The Brickyard so fast his knuckles stayed white for a good 20 minute afterwards. He'd bought her the watch soon after that. A man's watch – far too big and heavy to sit around her wrists without sliding off, and far too precious to drop in the ocean that way. She pulled it out of her bag and examined its cool, white face.

"7:30!" She said the time out loud. "That can't be…" Ellie shook her head. She was on English time now, and she suddenly felt a long way from Indiana.

Back home, her mother would be getting ready for her shift sorting parts at the Cole Motor Company; the newspaper boy would be setting up his stack of Stars on the road in front of their tenement like he always did; and the smell of hot oil, sweet pancakes and bacon would be drifting through the sash window from the canteen that backed onto their small yard. England didn't even smell the same. She felt something tug at her, from deep in her chest. She wished she'd never come. She should have just sent back a telegram of condolence and apologies. She didn't even know Lord Melmersby, and anyway Bertie had broken off the engagement without any real explanation, they had never married, and she had no connection to the family.

"No!" She spoke aloud to herself again. "Come on Ellie, it's an adventure. Pull yourself together." She straightened her wet jacket out purposefully, as though she were pulling herself straight with it. She was here now, it was a chance to see England, to see a different country, a different life. She wasn't the sort of woman who turned down a chance like that. She wouldn't allow herself to be.

She turned her head around the corner of the train shed to squint again at the tower clock on the pier, turning the dial to match her time to its 12:32 and dropping the heavy watch back into the small bag. The rain had eased off now, and the other travellers who had found temporary shelter under the eaves all along the way to the station doors began to move off again. Ellie clicked her bag shut and pulled firmly at the trolley handle.

"Right," she said. "I suppose I should go and see what Bertie's big brother is all about."

CHAPTER 2

"YOU must be Miss Eleanor Blaine."

It should have been a question, but it was spoken with a tone of certainty that didn't invite any answer but 'yes'.

"I am. And you must be Richard." Ellie put out her hand. The tall, stern-faced man who had just stepped off the train duly ignored it in favour of a stiff nod. "How did you know it was me?"

He looked her up and down, his expression answering for him as he examined her: boots, trousers, worn leather jacket and all.

"You can call me Dr Lindley," he said.

She smiled diplomatically. "And you can call me Ellie. Not even my mom calls me Eleanor. Well, unless I'm in trouble she doesn't."

He had already turned away, pulling up her trunk with one hand then turning his head back to nod her forward after him.

"It's a quick turnaround," he said, nodding his head in the direction of the front of the train. "They're changing the engine then it's straight back to London. Come!"

The way he barked the last word reminded her of how her father's boss, Harry Oppermeir, would call his bulldog when it was chewing the tyres of one of the racing cars her father was working on. Only with less affection in his voice.

"Nice to meet you too," Ellie said just a little too loudly to herself.

"Sorry?"

"Nothing." She smiled to herself. "Let's hit the rails."

Dr Lindley pulled sharply at the door of the Pullman carriage and put out a firm arm to help Ellie aboard. She took it with a nod of thanks and settled down into the padded seat, as her travel companion hoisted the heavy trunk into the overhead compartment and settled himself neatly down a little way off opposite to her. He straightened out his already immaculately pressed trousers and coughed slightly.

"We shall make sure you have all you need at Melmersby, of course," he said. "We'll need to get you some appropriate, um…" He looked awkwardly at Ellie and she followed his eyes as they ran over her outfit again.

"I'm sure it'll be very appropriate," she said. "I can't imagine it will be anything other than appropriate."

Richard coughed again and pulled out a copy of The Times from the shoulder bag he carried. Just large enough to hide behind.

The carriages were recoupled with a new engine and, after a short flurry of banging doors, tearful parting kisses of couples at windows, and daring children standing in the vents of steam that blasted the platform from the undercarriage, the train pulled out of the station with their cabin in silence, but for the rattle of the wheels on the track.

As they moved out of the sprawling dock city and into the countryside, Ellie could see a little of the England she had expected. Soft, tumbles of low hills dotted with sheep, cottages and canal boats; everything a richer, deeper green than she had ever seen before. Richard stayed behind the walls of his paper fort as the fields and forests rolled by, until at last the first rows of brick houses and factories rose up to usher them into the bustle and business of London.

At Paddington they'd taken the Underground. She'd ridden the Subway in New York a few times, but still felt a thrill at the thought of moving so fast beneath the earth. She looked to Richard for some sign he might be enjoying it, or for any sign of emotion at all – even curiosity about the woman his brother had been engaged to. Anything. By the time they had boarded the train from King's Cross

Station that would take them to York, Ellie had had enough.

"Ah, so that's what you look like!" she said. He looked annoyed; that much was clear. Probably about the mess she'd made of his newspaper by half-splitting it as she pulled it down from in front of his face. "I would think you'd have read the ink off the pages by now – there can't be that much interesting that happened in England on a Friday."

Richard pulled at the crumpled pages, trying to straighten out the broadsheet before giving up and folding it messily to put on the empty seat by his side. "I was writing a letter to the editor!" he snapped.

"Without a pen?"

"I was doing it in my head."

Ellie let out a quiet, sharp laugh. "Well, Bertie did say you were the brains of the family. Not so much the chatty one though, are you?"

Richard scowled, and Ellie leaned forward to force a look into his face. "Come on, we've been travelling half the day now and you've barely said a word. You were kind enough to pay for me to come over here, but I have no idea why, and you have no idea who you paid for. Perhaps we could exchange information? It would certainly liven up the journey."

Richard sniffed slightly. "I'm sorry, yes I've not been the most stimulating company. I have a lot on my mind right now. With my father, and I just had some troubling news from Melmersby before I left

London, a little trouble at the house which I could do without right now. But you're right, I quite forgot my manners. It's a pleasure to meet you."

Ellie shook her head. "No, I'm sorry. Of course, you've just lost your father. I know how that feels. I should have thought. Of course you're not in the mood to…"

"We weren't close." Richard waved away Ellie's apology with a flick of his long fingers.

"Oh," Ellie said. "I'm sorry to hear that. I'm sure it's not an easy time for you either way."

Richard didn't respond and they sank back into the uneasy silence that had been their mutual companion since Southampton. Ellie decided she wouldn't wait to dismiss it this time.

"Did you say trouble at the house? Nothing too bad I hope?"

He shook his head. "A break-in."

"Oh," Ellie exclaimed. "I hope they didn't take…"

"Nothing much. A silver cup and an old fountain pen," he said, cutting her short. "No harm done. All mended."

Ellie thought his face looked more troubled than his words allowed, but decided not to press him on it. "Thanks so much for inviting me, and for your generosity in paying my way over. That was pretty unexpected, and very kind of you."

Richard scratched at his broad forehead, furrowing it slightly as if in thought for a moment. "Don't thank me. I'm simply doing what I know

Bertie would have wanted. I did it for him, not you – I don't wish to appear rude but it matters not a jot to me whether you are at the service or not, I don't know the first thing about you, and I'm sure I care less. But I do know Bertie would have wanted you to say your goodbyes."

Ellie wondered what he sounded like when he did wish to appear rude. "I'm not sure why Bertie would want me to say goodbye to his father? I never met him, and all I know about him is that he hated the idea of Bertie's relationship with me. I hope you haven't troubled yourself to bring me over on mistaken information?"

Richard straightened his back. "Not to say goodbye to father, to say goodbye to Bertie."

It was Ellie's turn now to be silent.

"Father would never have wanted you at the Hall, and I was in no position to make your case on Bertie's behalf while he was alive, even had I wanted to. Father has been laid to rest in the family tomb, beside Bertie. I think that at least you deserve the opportunity to say goodbye to my brother properly. I know it is what Bertie would have wanted."

Ellie felt a hot tear rise and tried to push it back with the base of her hand, holding it in place as she spoke. "Thank you." She forced a smile. "Though you must know Bertie broke the engagement? He was very sweet about it, but I wasn't his fiancée when he died. Perhaps I shouldn't have been there for him anyway?"

Richard's stern face fell slightly, and for just a moment Ellie thought she could see a little of the man she had known in his brother – the eyes were the same, just darker; in every way. "I was with him. When he died. So I can assure you I know exactly what he wanted."

The train whistle shook them from themselves with a sharp retort. Richard's face rearranged itself back into its usual sternness and he picked up his crumpled Times. "Right, York Station. Here we are. Best be on our way."

Ellie nodded. For the first time since she'd waved goodbye to Bertie at the docks in New York all those years ago, she felt he was close by her again now. She let the tear fall at last.

ELLIE BLAINE 1920s MYSTERIES

CHAPTER 3

"THAT'S a Sunbeam isn't it? 24? I heard they were introducing a sports model with a 24-valve overhead camshaft engine. Does it have the Claudel Hobson carburetor?"

Richard and the man with the car looked at each and shrugged.

"The Claudel Hobson? Or does it still have the SU? Is it this year's model?" Ellie glanced from one to the other. "No?"

"I'm afraid you might as well be talking Chinese to him," the man said, nodding at Richard, who raised his eyebrow sharply in response. "He don't know the first thing about cars. And me, I just drive 'em, polish 'em, and sometimes tinker to keep 'em going. I don't care too much for Claude

Whatsits or how many valves. Long as they run well, an engine is an engine to me."

"Thank you, Malkie," Richard said. "Mr Fawthrop here was Lord Melmersby's driver for… how long has it been now, Malkie?"

The man put back the peaked cap he'd taken off to address Ellie. "Twenty five years, right out of the Army. And I am still his driver, as you well know, sir, and as I shall be 'till I can't drive no more."

Ellie wasn't sure, but it sounded more like an order than an observation, and she detected more than a little tension in the air as the two men addressed each other.

"So you keep reminding me, Malkie. So how about you do what Lord Melmersby's driver should do and help a lady with her luggage."

Malkie's eyes narrowed for a second, then opened wide as he stepped stiffly over to retrieve Ellie's case.

"That's ok, I've got it," she insisted, but the driver half-pulled it from her grip in his keenness to help.

"No problem at all miss, can't have a young lady like yourself hauling about a great heavy case like this, doing yourself a mischief."

Ellie observed that a plump, bow-legged driver who walked with a limp and must be far more than twice her age was the more likely of the two of them to do any damage to themselves, but she kept a straight face as she stepped back to allow him to wheezily secure the trunk to the runner of the car.

"Is it far to Melmersby from here?" she asked.

"About 30 miles," Richard said. "We should be there in about an hour, a little more maybe?"

"An hour!" Ellie said, incredulously. "To go 30 miles? If you let me drive I'll have us there in half that time."

"Now miss," Malkie said, removing his cap again, "it's not my place but I'm not sure it would be right for a young lady like yourself…"

"Stuff and nonsense!" Richard said, smiling for the first time since Ellie had seen him – though with a touch of devilry in it, she thought. "It's 1921 for God's sake – I'm sure Miss Blaine is a very capable driver and it will do you good to rest your old bones on the way back."

Malkie glanced nervously at the car as though Richard had just ordered him to hand over his first born to a complete stranger. He looked upset, which may just have been the whole purpose in Richard agreeing to it, Ellie thought.

"Very well, sir." The last word was spat more than it was spoken. "Step this way miss, I shall run through a few instructions for you."

"No need!" Ellie beamed, hurdling the door to land in the driver's seat. "You've got everything on the wrong side of the car, but I'm sure it works just the same as any I've driven back home."

* * *

"Perhaps you should be keeping your eyes on the road? Just a suggestion." Richard's voice was shaking, and she wasn't sure if it was from the judder of the car on the rough tarmac, or if it was related to how white his face had now gone and how tightly he was holding on to his hat.

"Don't worry, it's a straight run here. This car's got a decent bit of poke to it, hasn't it?" Ellie turned to Malkie, who had given up on his own hat now and ducked down in the front passenger seat to keep the wind from blowing away any more of his thinning, grey hair.

"Some of the cars they race back home have a little mirror at the front so you can see behind you," she shouted above the rushing air. "That would make it easier to talk, don't you think?"

She turned back to Richard again and he shook his head firmly.

"Is he always like this in the car, Malkie?" she asked the slouched figure in the shotgun seat.

"Dunno miss, I never driven him this fast. His father wouldn't have minded though, he weren't scared of nothing, I'll tell you that much."

Ellie turned back to see Richard's reaction, but this time it wasn't nerves she saw, but what looked very much like anger.

His face darkened and she could see his teeth grinding, locking his firm jaw closed against whatever it was he thought to say.

She wasn't sure how it worked with the English aristocracy and their staff, but she began to have the feeling the relationship between these two men wasn't typical.

"My father was a fool," Richard snapped back at Malkie – his clenched jaw no longer enough to hold back his words. "If he wasn't, you wouldn't even be in this car."

Ellie looked quickly from one to the other. No, this definitely wasn't how she expected two such men to talk to each other.

"Your father was wise enough to know who really cared about 'im, and wise enough to see 'em right before he died, and you cain't do nothin' about that – that's one thing you can't take away from me at least." Malkie turned to Ellie, all the time throwing darts of a sideways glance at Richard. "He's Lord Melmersby now, but the real one gave me this job for life. It's all legal and everything, Lady Melmersby saw to that, God bless her. But his father gave me a lot more than that too and he knows it. Maybe ask him about that. What about that then?"

Richard went to speak again, but now Ellie had decided the atmosphere was disintegrating even faster than the car was going – and she would have to flip that on its head.

"In the name of God, Miss Blaine!" Richard had his hat pressed down flat against his head now. "Slow the damn car down!"

Ellie laughed, and wished she did have a rear-view mirror in this car so she could get a proper look at Richard's face now.

Malkie smirked to himself, but then put his hand on the dash and turned to Ellie. "He's right mind, miss. There's a real sharp turn coming up – you 'ave to take it almost walking pace, there's scarce room to go round, even a driver like you."

She squeezed the brakes, quietly pleased with what she took as a compliment. The road turned hard to the left and to the side, half-buried in spring flowers and fresh stalks of meadow grass, was a sign that simply read: *'Melmersby'*.

"Corner's 'ere, miss – just by the duck pond."

Malkie was right, the road banked more steeply to the left than she'd realised, almost doubling back on itself. Ellie's foot pumped sharply on the brakes and she felt the back wheels get away from her slightly as she was forced to let the car run with the skid to straighten itself up just before it hit the verge. A brace of ducks flew sharply up, startled by the sound of screeching rubber and cursing voices.

"Damn it Miss Blaine!" Richard growled. "Take a little care will you, you almost had us in the pond."

Ellie reddened. She'd managed the skid expertly, but she couldn't deny she's got them in it in the first place.

"I tried to tell you, din' I?" Malkie muttered. "You're not on a racetrack here."

Ellie took the rest of the drive at a steadier pace through Melmersby, which looked just like an English village should, she thought; from the ducks on the pond, to the gingham-curtained tea-shop, the cow-grazed green and the sharp steeple of a stumpy, old church. She smiled to herself, quickly forgetting her embarrassment.

"Up here, Miss Blaine – just past the grand old oak on your left." Richard indicated to where the road opened up to allow a car to turn in. They passed under an arch of pale yellow stone, the footprint of a building still marked in stone in the earth where a gatehouse would once have stood. The gravel of a long, tree-lined driveway crackled under the tires as they turned into sight of Melmersby Hall itself.

"Quite a place you've got here." Ellie beamed.

Richard grunted half-hearted acknowledgement. He would have said that it was a small affair compared to some of the great houses of Yorkshire; that the whole building would fit in a single wing of a place like Harewood House, but he supposed to someone from Indianapolis it would appear very grand. The house itself was built of the same yellow stone that made up the entrance arch. The sharp gables of two wings flanked a central hall lit up with two tiers of tall sash windows, in the centre of which was the angled arch of the main entrance below an elaborate, iron-railed balcony.

"It's been in the family since 1584," Richard said, matter-of-factly. "So it's older than your country." He laughed weakly at his own comment then coughed quietly when it got no response. "Most of what you see was built about 150 years ago. It's falling apart, of course. Costs a fortune to run. Half of it is uninhabitable. Father was just too stubborn and sentimental about it to leave, of course – seemed to believe it would break his ancestors' hearts if he did. Funny how he cared so much for the feelings of the dead, and so little for the living, when it came to family."

His voice petered out at the last, and his cough returned, along with a flushing of his cheeks that suggested to Ellie he may have said more than he meant to.

The imposing front door, which was already slightly ajar as the car pulled in, now swung fully open to reveal the figure of a round-faced, ruddy-cheeked woman who was busily untangling herself from an apron which she quickly, but carefully, folded and placed neatly on the lintel before stepping over the thin verge of close-cut grass that lined the walls of the house and trotted towards the car.

"That's Mrs Madison," Malkie said quietly. "Best stay on her good side, she's not the kind to hold her tongue when she has something to say about a'body."

Ellie imagined from what she'd seen so far that nobody here was that kind. "Is she the housekeeper?"

"Housekeeper, cook, butler – gardener sometimes – the Melmersbys never 'ave been ones to spend a pound when a shilling gets the work done. Sorry to say." He looked up to the heavens with those last words.

"Mrs Madison!" Richard smiled broadly and Ellie raised her eyebrows in surprise that he had that good humour in him for anyone. "I hope all has been well? And are you alright – with everything?"

Mrs Madison, who had looked as calm and steady as anyone could on first coming out of the house, now suddenly put on a display of concern and worry that Ellie thought wouldn't look out of place in one of the sensational melodramas she'd seen at the Circle Theatre back home. "Oh, now Richard, it quite gave me the vapours! To think some villain was in the house while me and little Lucy was here all alone with just Mr Madison to take care of us. We heard him clattering about, we did, middle of the night, fair shook us both up. I feel quite weak at the knees just thinking about it."

Mrs Madison's knees looked very sturdy, Ellie thought. And was it just her or did no-one here speak to Lord Melmersby as though he were a lord? That suited her just fine, but still she found it a little odd, especially given all she had heard of his illustrious family from Bertie.

"And is Mr Madison well?" Richard asked softly.

"As well as can be, sir. As well as can be."

"Excellent!" Richard said, then stepped back to gesture Ellie forward. "This is Miss Eleanor Blaine, she will be staying with us for a while. Be sure to take good care of her. Perhaps you could show her to her room and Malkie shall help with the bags."

Mrs Madison stepped forward, her plump face that

had been dimpled with unalloyed joy as she talked to Richard now fell, shiny cheeks reshaping themselves into begrudging jowls in an instant. "Miss Blaine," she said, with the faintest of nods.

Ellie did her best to present a more friendly expression, but it seemed to have little effect on Mrs Madison who gruffly gestured her to follow as Malkie took up her case from the car. She followed the housekeeper-cum-butler through the arch of the doorway and into the hall. The ceiling was lower than she had expected, and coated with a sparsely-decorated pattern of plasterwork. The walls were panelled with light oak, and in the centre of the far wall a small fire burned in a vast stone fireplace. If it gave out any heat, none of it seemed to reach this far into the room. Above it, the huge, scowling figure of a stern-faced man in black glared down from a gilded picture frame.

"My father," Richard said, following her eyes to where they fixed on the portrait. "Keeping an eye on everyone, even now."

Ellie detected little affection in his tone. She looked at the portrait again and shivered, only partly from the cold.

"We had a heating system put in a few years back," Richard said. "Your room should be a little more comfortable – these big old rooms down here take some warming up. You get used to it."

Ellie nodded and Richard gestured through an arch in the wooden walls and towards a wide, winding staircase. "I just have to attend to something, but Mrs Madison will show you the way."

She thanked him and followed the housekeeper up the stairs, Malkie grunting and wheezing behind as he hauled her case up with him.

"Here you are. Make yourself comfortable. You will want to change before dinner," Mrs Madison said as she opened the door to what was to be Ellie's room. It sounded more like an order than a suggestion.

The room was pleasant enough, she thought, and Richard had been right about it being warmer; although the cold draft blowing through the gaps in the ill-fitting sash window meant you needed to be careful where you stood to remain warm for long. The bed was as wide as her own bed at home was long, and creaked loudly as Ellie sat down on it; but the mattress was comfortable and the sheets were thick.

Beside the bed, a pitcher of water, floated with ice and fresh mint leaves, stood on a glass-topped mahogany table. Ellie poured herself a drink to wash away the dust of the road from her throat and looked around the room.

Each wall held a portrait: a man riding a horse while holding a sword aloft on one; the time-darkened, foreboding scowls of some very serious-looking men in wide ruff-collars on two others. Directly opposite her bed, beside the window, was a smaller portrait that caught Ellie's eye. A young man – by the look of the clothes it might have been painted when Queen Victoria was still a girl – stood with his hand on his hip, a small, eager-looking dog at his heels and a mischievous smile that made this portrait as bright as the others were dark. The man, some long-gone relative no doubt, had that same familiar, light, almost strawberry-blond, hair that she remembered running her fingers through; that same sense of unfettered life and energy.

She smiled to herself, feeling somewhere halfway between sadness and joy. She looked away and out of the window to where she could see Malkie now putting away the Sunbeam in the green-double-doored, stone building just opposite.

"My bag!" she shouted. She'd left her clutch bag in the car; she'd need that before Malkie locked the car away for the evening. Hastily putting on the boots she'd only just pulled off she dashed out into the corridor – suddenly unsure where she had come in by.

"Left?" she thought to herself. "No right. No, left." She turned sharply round the corner, carefully avoiding the low table that held a vase she was sure she couldn't afford to replace if she broke it, and ran – almost straight into the door that was now opening in front of her to the sound of muttered curses.

"Damn you! What the Hell were they– oh, I'm so sorry Miss Blaine, I didn't see you there."

"Richard – sorry, I was just… I was trying to get my bag. It's still in the car."

She was suddenly aware of just how tall he was, up

so close. She straightened out her shirt and forced a smile. "I just need to… my bag…"

"I shall have Malkie bring it in," Richard said, slowly closing the door behind him.

Ellie tried to catch a furtive glance into the room Richard had just been cursing at, as the door closed. "Is everything alright?" she said.

"Absolutely fine," Richard said abruptly. "I was just inspecting the damage from the break-in. Nothing major. They must have been disturbed before they did too much harm."

"Well I'm glad it's not too bad," Ellie said. "Perhaps Mr Madison saw them off?"

Richard laughed in a way that surprised her. "Well, perhaps he did. He's rather intimidating when he needs to be. Goodnight, Miss Blaine."

Ellie tipped her head to return the pleasantry. It had been a long trip, and nothing she had seen since she arrived had been as she expected it to be. But it would be interesting, she knew that; and 'interesting' was definitely something she could feel at home with.

ELLIE BLAINE 1920s MYSTERIES

Chapter 4

ELLIE woke with a start to the clatter of bone china on a glass-topped bedside table.

"I am so sorry, Miss Blaine, I wasn't sure whether to wake you or not, you were dead to the world. I expect it must have been a long old trip for you?"

Ellie rubbed her eyes, trying hard to focus on the figure who was now busying herself with tying back the curtains from the sash window. The morning light forced her eyes closed again as hard as she tried to open them. She shook her head to clear the cobwebs that seemed to have wrapped themselves around it.

"That's alright," she said. "I think I must have gone out like a light last night, I don't even remember going to sleep. I'm sorry about the mess, I should have put my things away."

The woman gave a nervous laugh, and as Ellie's eyes began to find their focus she could see she was much younger than Mrs Madison, maybe three or four years younger than herself, with glossy black hair and a delicately pretty face that seemed unnaturally crumpled right now with concern.

"Oh don't you worry about that, that's what I'm here for," she said, playing awkwardly with her fingers. "I'm so, so very sorry that I'm so late – I'm afraid there's only me and Mrs Madison and she's not feeling so well and she's only just got out of bed herself. I've got quite behind on my chores. I am doing my best to keep up but Rich... Lord Melmersby might need to get some more... I mean it's not my place, but there's only two of us and..."

The woman's voice faded out and Ellie turned over to fumble with the clutch bag that Malkie had brought up just before she fell asleep. She barely remembered him passing it awkwardly through the narrow opening of the door, looking the other way in case she was not in a 'fit state' to be seen. "It's just gone seven," Ellie said wearily, looking at her watch. "What time do you usually have breakfast here?"

The young woman turned quickly to look at Ellie, then broke into a smile that seemed to signal relief. "Just past seven? Are you sure? Oh, thank goodness. I'm not doing so bad. Mrs Madison can get awful fierce you see, if I don't keep things tight and 'Bristol fashion' like she tells me."

Ellie nodded and swung her legs over the side of the bed, still fighting the tiredness that seemed to grip her whole body. She tipped the small teapot, decorated with exquisitely painted pink pastel blossoms and brown branches, to pour out its contents into a matching, delicate teacup.

"That's Mrs Madison's favourite," the girl said, nodding at the pot. "Her special pick-me-up fruit tea recipe, she thought you might need it after such a long trip."

Ellie took a deep sip, then threw her head back a little, eyes opening wide. "Whoa! It's a pick-me-up alright! It's got quite a kick."

The woman blushed. "Yes, there's a drop of her plum brandy in it. She says it does wonders for the constitution."

Ellie raised the glass, and her eyebrows. "Well, it's a little early for me, especially on a Sunday – but 'when in England' I suppose." She took a deeper draught and shook her head. It certainly seemed to do the trick, although she thought she wouldn't make a habit of it.

"Now, when you look in the wardrobe, Lord Melmersby made sure to buy some clothes for you, so as you would have the right dress for dinner and the service and such," the woman said. "On account of what his brother told him of you, he said that I should pick them out as I would be a good fit for them so as to make sure they fit you, but you can have them adjusted if you need to, by Mrs Lorimer what does the dressmaking in the village."

"I'm sure they'll be perfect as they are," Ellie said. "Sorry, I've been rude – I haven't asked your name?"

"Lucy, miss. Lucy Madison at your service. They are lovely dresses, miss, and I feel a little ashamed to say I did enjoy trying them on. I hope you don't mind. Only I am sure you will look so much prettier in them than I did."

Ellie stood up, feeling the blood rush a little to her head as she did. "Don't be silly," she said gently. "I should imagine you looked a doll in them – I'm sure you've probably broken every heart in the village by now, haven't you?'

Lucy blushed. "I wouldn't say that Miss Blaine. Anyhow, I'll just clear up if you've finished." She went to pick up the tea set, then glanced down at the watch on the table, then at Ellie. "That's a very handsome watch, miss. Is it American? It's very big. It's just, Bertie would always say everything is so much bigger in America. Is it, miss? I'd love to go to America."

Ellie laughed softly and looked around the room. "Well, the houses are certainly a lot bigger in England."

"May I try it on, miss?" Lucy said, reaching for the watch then quickly pulling her hand back as if it had been put on a hot pan. "Oh my, I'm so sorry, I don't know my place sometimes."

Ellie smiled and handed the watch to her. "Don't be silly, there are no 'places' in my room. Here, try it on."

The heavy watch hung even more loosely over Lucy's delicate wrist than it did on Ellie's, and she pulled it further up her forearm before taking it off and turning it over in her hand to inspect more closely. "Oh, there's an inscription on the back. Am I allowed to read it?"

Ellie nodded.

Lucy cupped the watch in her small hand, moving over to the open window to better catch the soft morning light on its surface, then running a finger over the inscribed words. *"To the fastest girl in town – I count the time until you speed your way back to me. B."*

Lucy's face crumpled in thought for just a second, then she turned back suddenly to Ellie. "Oh gosh, it was a present from Bertie! I am so sorry, I shouldn't have…"

"It's alright. He bought it for me when he had to leave for England. It's a driver's watch – so I could time myself when I took my father's old car for a run, he said."

"I'm so sorry for what happened, miss. I can't imagine the heartbreak."

Ellie shook her head. "I'm not the only one who had my heart broken by that awful war,.And time is meant to heal us, right? I still have all the time left in that watch, and it does get a little better…" She felt something rise up in herself she wasn't ready to show right now. "Anyway, talking of time – I suppose you should see to the other rooms before Mrs Madison comes looking for you."

"Oh, of course. Mustn't get in trouble," Lucy said, standing sharply and handing her back the watch to tuck safely in the bag. Ellie smiled a thank you and Lucy blushed again, before gathering up the crockery from the table and holding it close to her white linen pinny, taking care not to let it spill. She stopped just before the door. "We all miss Bertie, miss," she said. "He was the sweetest gentleman you could ever meet and he spoke ever so well of you."

Ellie looked up and saw that Lucy's eyes sparkled with the same water she was still trying to hold back herself. "You know, I think he told me about you too," Ellie said. "He mentioned there was a girl who worked in the house and that you were thick as thieves when you were children. I suppose you must be Mrs Madison's daughter? I'm sorry, I'm so groggy I didn't make the connection when you told me your name."

"That's quite alright," Lucy said. "Well, Mrs Madison is my aunt. Sort of. But more like a mother. In a way. My mother died having me, you see and she – Mrs Madison – she was the closest to her and she never had no children of her own, nor got married, so she sort of took me in. I call her mum, though. When she's in a good mood. Which is not that often... I should probably go."

Ellie frowned. "She's not married? What about Mr Madison?"

Lucy giggled. "Oh, no. Everyone calls her Mrs Madison on account of Mr Madison. But they aren't married. You can't have met him yet then?" Her giggle grew until it caught up in Ellie's throat too and she found herself laughing along, without really knowing why.

Lucy wiped a tear from her eye with the edge of her pinny. "You must make sure that you get on the good side of Mr Madison," she said in a tone of mock-seriousness. 'Your standing in the household is very much dependent on his approval or otherwise of your person! That's what Mrs Madison says."

Ellie raised a puzzled brow. "I shall make sure I do. I–"

Lucy smiled again and left the room with a respectful bob of her head, a playful curl still playing on her lips as she closed the door. Ellie rubbed her eyes, suddenly aware of how tired she still felt. She bit the corner of one of the pieces of buttered toast, then lay back into the thick nest of pillows and closed her eyes.

* * *

She woke again with a start to the sound of a woman screaming.

"What on earth was that?" Ellie said, jolting upwards, taking just a second to look around the room and remember where she was. The woman screamed again and now she heard the sound of footsteps on gravel, running. She threw her legs over the side of the bed, and stood up, her head still so full of fog she felt dizzy at the sudden standing and nearly had to sit down again. She shook out her head and stepped towards the sash window. Outside she could see Richard with an older woman who was wailing and clinging to his jacket as he gingerly put an arm around her shoulder.

Ellie hastily pulled on the same trousers she'd worn the night before, which were folded across the top of her bedside chair, and wrapped her jacket around her shoulders, still wearing her nightdress beneath. She pulled open the door and quickly turned into the corridor towards the top of the wide staircase that led down into the entrance hall. She gripped the smooth top of the carved banisters that ran down the stairs, steadying herself at a trot down into the hall, to be met by Richard, his face as dark as his father's portrait, walking back into the house and towards her.

"Ah, there you are. Could I ask that you please stay in your room? I'm afraid there has been the most distressing accident."

Ellie looked around his broad shoulder as he blocked her way, trying to get a picture of what was going on outside. She could see the small, grey-haired woman sat on her haunches in the gravel, Mrs Madison and Lucy now either side of her with their arms around her back as it rose and fell in heavy sobs.

"What on earth has happened?" Ellie said.

"It's Malkie," Richard said, looking back over his shoulder. "It seems he was working under the car when… when something must have slipped. The poor man. I was too late to help him."

Ellie felt her chest tighten, shaking her head as much in grim certainty as confusion.

Richard turned back to look towards the door, then put a hand to Ellie's arm. "I'm afraid poor Malkie is dead."

ELLIE BLAINE 1920s MYSTERIES

CHAPTER 5

"HE was a nice enough fella, used to run me into the village sometimes when I needed to pick up something for the kitchen or get my cards read by Madame Zuzu. She's very good with the cards, you know. She learned it all from a travelling gypsy she had a wild affair with as a young woman. That's what she says anyway. Her name's Dorothy really, not Zuzu. Dot, her old man calls her. Not that she reads much these days, what with her varicose veins she can't sit still too long. Anyway she's good with the cards. She told me I was an Egyptian princess in a previous life and, do you know, I think she's right; I feel very much at home with my toes in the sand at Scarborough beach and I never told her that, so how did she know? She's very good."

Ellie nodded, still poised ready for a pause long enough to speak. She made this the fifth pause so far, but – like the others before – it wasn't quite long enough.

"Of course his poor wife will be beside herself. Is it any surprise? Now she's not someone I know too well. She's not from round here of course. Family from Otley way. They say her father was a drunk who spent his life in front of or behind bars of one kind or another. And from what I gather – well, like-father-like-daughter they do say. Not that I'd speak ill of her, what with what just happened, of course."

Mrs Madison stopped for breath, just long enough this time.

"Did Richard mention how it happened? What was he doing under the car?"

Ellie was still feeling more than a little put out that Richard had ushered her into the 'care' of Mrs Madison while he saw to events in the garage. The police had been called, as well as an ambulance from the hospital at Harrogate, while Lucy had taken Mrs Fowthrop home. Not that she would have been able to do much – poor Malkie was well past that – but she had seen her share of accidents at the race track since she was in pigtails and wasn't sure she liked the thought that Richard might think her too 'delicate' to deal with one here.

She was even more put out that Richard had caught the whiff of plum brandy on her breath as they spoke and commented about the early hour.

She wasn't sure now if Mrs Madison hadn't planned it that way, as she was getting the distinct impression the housekeeper was not too keen on her presence in the house.

"Well your guess is as good as mine," Mrs Madison said, pushing her thick-fingered hand deep into a well-buttered chicken to deposit a bunch of fragrant thyme. "He was always very careful was Malkie; meticulous to a fault, dear Lady Melmersby used to say." She pushed her hand in even deeper. "I did hear the police officer say the most curious thing though. Seems he had a feather in his hand when they found him. Perhaps he were distracted by one of the chickens. They get in there sometimes and make a right mess. I tell Lucy to keep the chicken shed door shut, but she's got cloth for ears sometimes, that girl." She pushed her hand in even further, and grimaced.

"A feather?"

'Aye, a white one. Mind, all the chickens are red so who knows what to think. Terrible business, really." She pulled her hand out again and glared at the stuffed bird with a look of satisfaction, before turning to face Ellie and wiping her hands on a faded dish cloth. "I suspect with all these goings-on you shan't be with us for too long. I'd imagine you'll be keen to get back to America, won't you? Perhaps straight after the service. We shall have to get another driver, of course, to run you back to York. Maybe Richard will do it. I shall speak to him about it if you wish."

"I'm sure something will be arranged," Ellie said, trying her best to keep her tone at least neutral. "I shouldn't imagine I will stay much longer than that."

Mrs Madison threw up her sturdy arms in an exaggerated show of concern. "Oh, of course dear – we are not trying to run you off. Oh dear, no." Her hollow laughter did little to convince Ellie of her sincerity, but she decided not to push it further.

The latch on the kitchen door clicked open and Ellie turned, expecting to see Richard or Lucy walk in and to be able to press them for more information on Malkie's unfortunate demise. Instead, the wiry figure of a gaunt-faced man, dressed in faded tweed with a tattered cloth cap on his head, stepped through – a bundle of rabbit and a rather bloody pheasant slung over his arm. He was a young man, Ellie observed, though it took her a moment to realise that, as his thin, drawn face seemed to carry the look of cares beyond his years.

"I am sorry, M..Mrs M..Madison. I din' know yer 'ad c...comp'ny. I shall get me gone."

"Don't be silly, Jim. Sit down right now. And don't stutter so." She turned to Ellie. "He stutters awfully when he's nervous and he's nervous around strange ladies. Aren't you, Jim?"

Jim didn't speak.

"Don't mind me, I'm pretty harmless. The name's Ellie," she said, standing up to put out her hand in greeting. Jim ignored it and kept his eyes on the game he had placed on the heavy wooden table top. She could see his hands were shaking. "Do you need something, Jim? A coffee maybe? I could—"

"He's fine," Mrs Madison said. "You're fine, aren't you, Jim?"

The man nodded.

"Got a bit shaken up in the war, didn't you, Jimmy? Not been quite right since. Jim lives up by the woods at Melmersby Top, takes care of the grounds and the game, don't you lad? Very good shot but the noise sets him off and gets him all to shaking. I'll fix you up a little fruit tea, one of my specials – that always calms you down, doesn't it, love?"

Jim shook his head silently and Mrs Madison put back the bottle she had pulled from the high shelf of a dresser, stopping just a second to take a quick sip before popping the cork back in.

"Course Jim was in the same regiment as Bertie, weren't you, love? Was there with him when... well, when it happened."

Ellie looked curiously at Jim, hoping for a moment she might get to ask him more about what happened that day. All she knew was that Bertie died in action, and that he'd been awarded a Military Cross for the price of his life. Her requests to the family for more information had gone unanswered, just like all the letters and telegrams she sent. But she wouldn't get any answers today; Jim was clearly not in the mood for talking.

"Well, I shall b...be off, Mrs Madison. Just came to drop these bits off for you, I shouldn't stay.

T…terrible business here. Mother will have seen 'em police cars down the lane and I should go and see to her 'case she's worryin'. Good day to you now. Antyoumiss.' He mumbled the last words one into each other, touching his cap and keeping his eyes to the floor as he shuffled out the way he had come in.

"Of course I should know not to bring up Bertie when he is here, what was I thinking?" Mrs Madison said, wiping down her hands on her apron as the door clicked behind him. "He looked up to Bertie so, did Jim. Master Bertie made him his batman, you know – proud as Punch he was about that. Well, everyone looked up to Bertie. We always thought he would make a fine Lord Melmersby – find himself a nice, well-connected lady and carry on the family line. He could have had his pick of the very best society ladies, of course. His poor mother was always hoping he'd meet someone suitable, but she was always disappointed, we all were. I suppose that's just – oh, now who could that be?"

The clank of the brass doorbell broke Mrs Madison's ramblings, leaving Ellie a little unsure whether the housekeeper had picked her words clumsily, or just as precisely as she wished. She shook her head, looking around the kitchen at the spotless surfaces, neatly stacked plates and immaculately polished glassware. No, Mrs Madison was not one to put anything where she didn't mean it to go. She wasn't about to stay somewhere she wasn't wanted, and besides, she's heard the ambulance leave at least 10 minutes ago, so there wouldn't be anything for Richard to 'protect' her from now. She stood up to leave, but as she reached for the door it swung open ahead of her to reveal a smartly dressed young woman; small, black-rimmed glasses perched on a thin nose and a broad smile across her angular face as she leaned eagerly into the room.

"Ah! The American girl! How absolutely delightful to meet you. I am here to save you. You can thank me later."

Mrs Madison firmly, but carefully, stepped around the woman to pass through the door first and reclaim her kitchen. "Miss Blaine, may I introduce Miss Georgina Parr. She has come calling for you. As you can see." Ellie subtly smiled to herself at the sudden forced refinement in Mrs Madison's voice – imagining this must be her 'butler' tone that she saved for guests.

"You can call me Georgie, everyone does," the woman said briskly, stepping into the room and setting herself down on one of the high stools that stood against the central table. "When I heard what had happened, and that Richard had locked up his guest like Rapunzel in the tower, well, I just had to come over and carry you off."

"That must make you Prince Georgie then?" Ellie said with a wry smile, which made the woman laugh and Mrs Madison frown.

"Especially when I heard you were Bertie's girl from America. How terribly exciting. As you can probably imagine, nothing exciting ever happens here. Apart from this ghastly business this morning, of course. I shall remove you to the drawing room and we shall open Dr Lindley's drinks cabinet and you will tell me all about America."

Georgie was certainly insistent, she thought, but she didn't need too much persuasion to step out of Mrs Madison's kitchen. "Sure. Let's get a drink – might as well carry on the day the way I started it."

"Super!" Georgie beamed. "I shall steal her from you then, Mrs Madison."

The housekeeper tightened the strings of her apron around her ample stomach, huffing slightly as she did. "That is all fine by me, Miss Parr. I have business to attend to and Mr Madison will be wanting his luncheon."

Georgie smiled. "And how is Mr Madison, these days? The last time I was here he was having a little trouble with his toileting?"

"Oh that's all cleared up now, I think it was the partridge. Too rich for him with the whisky sauce and all."

Ellie shot a curious glance, first at Georgie then at Mrs Madison as she pulled out a bundle of keys from under her apron to unlock the door of a small cupboard just to the side of the deep sink. Instantly, there was a rattling and a clatter from the side door of the kitchen that led out into the little walled herb garden, and then, from under the cabinet, a large, rather raggedy-looking and clearly very well fed, old ginger cat appeared, purring loudly and licking his lips.

"Ah, Mr Madison, there you are!" Georgie exclaimed.

"*That's* Mr Madison?" Ellie said, then let out a laugh. "Well, hello Mr Madison, nice to meet you."

Mr Madison looked up at Georgie, then at Ellie. Ignoring the cooing calls and outstretched arms of Mrs Madison, he scurried under the kitchen table to sniff at her boots, then rub his broad, furry cheeks against her ankle, before rolling over to show his impressive belly, and purring even more loudly.

Mrs Madison's face darkened and she quickly rattled the food cupboard keys to get him up and on his feet again and across the room in a flash.

Georgie laughed loudly. "Well, that is a first. Looks like Mr Madison has taken a shine to you. You shall simply have to stay at Melmersby now until he dismisses you."

Ellie smiled, and looked again at the cat, who was now wolfing down a pile of game trimmings and gravy. "At least someone seems to be glad I'm here," she thought.

ELLIE BLAINE 1920s MYSTERIES

CHAPTER 6

GEORGIE pulled the crystal stopper from the decanter she had taken off a dark oak and brass side cabinet. The amber liquid inside glistened with the late morning sunlight that broke through the still half-closed shutters of the drawing room, as she swirled it around and breathed in its aroma from the open top.

"Richard really needs to get more staff," she said. "Poor Lucy and Mrs Madison are rushed off their feet, and the place is never opened up in the day before it has to be closed down again at night." She poured two glasses, handing one to Ellie while she started on her own. "Ugh!" she grimaced. "And he needs to buy more whisky, this tastes like it's been sat here since before the war."

Ellie sniffed at her glass, before putting it down on the tablecloth that covered a large, very old-looking, table set against the wide window.

"So. You are the famous Ellie, then," Georgie said, looking her baffled subject up and down.

"I'm not sure I'm particularly–"

"Bertie told me everything about you," she chirped.

"Everything?" Ellie frowned.

"Oh, he did nothing but talk of you. Crashingly boring for everyone else of course, and I was fortunate to be one of the very select few who weren't madly in love with him, so I quite enjoyed his tales of the daring American beauty who stole his heart. Everyone else was utterly disappointed of course."

Ellie allowed herself a dry laugh. "I think Bertie may have been prone to tall tales about everything he saw in America. He was a very charming storyteller – he could always add a little spice where he thought it might liven things up a little."

"No – I won't hear it. I demand to hear tales of races won, hearts broken and showdowns at high noon with dark-eyed gunslingers."

Ellie laughed more heartily now. "There aren't too many cowboys in Indianapolis these days, I'm sorry to tell you. And I would race some of the test boys when the track was closed, but that was about it for my racing career. And I'm not sure how many hearts I've broken, but if I did I didn't notice them. So, sorry, I might not live up to the billing after all."

"Nonsense!" Georgie said firmly, pouring another whisky and pulling the same face again at its taste. "I want to hear everything about you, and I won't take no for an answer." Georgie patted the spare cushion of the two-seater leather sofa she had dropped herself down into, and Ellie sat down beside her, softly shaking her head to herself.

"What's to say?" Ellie said. "I'm just a fairly ordinary girl from Indiana."

"An ordinary girl who drives like a demon and stole the heart of the most eligible man in Yorkshire," Georgie interrupted.

"Well, I suppose I was lucky on both counts there. My father was a test driver and mechanic for Mr Oppermeir, who owned one of the big racing teams in town, and my mother works for Coles on the assembly line, so I suppose I have gasoline in my blood."

"How marvellous!" Georgie beamed. "And I like to think you captured Bertie's heart when he saw you tearing up the race track?"

Ellie sighed. "Not quite. After my father... well, there was a terrible flood in the city."

"You poor thing!" Georgie said, putting a sympathetic hand to Ellie's knee.

"It's alright. It was a long time ago, and time is meant to heal us, right?" Ellie said, not too convincingly. "After he died, I needed to help out a little, so I took a job at Drammer's – the motor dealership. I think Mr Drammer just wanted me to smile and flatter the gentlemen who came to look at the cars, but when I could – when he wasn't there – I would sometimes take them out for a test drive."

"Of course, I remember now," Georgie said, clapping her hands together. "Bertie said you fairly turned his hair grey, some great beast of a sports car – he swore you must have broken every record."

Ellie reddened slightly. "I may have been showing off a little, he was the first Englishman I'd met and I think I wanted to show him how we do things in the States."

Georgie clasped Ellie's hands between hers. "Well, it certainly worked – you impressed him alright."

She blushed further, then gently pulled her hands back. "Could I ask you something now?"

Georgie gulped down a slug of whisky. "Um… yes of course, darling. Anything."

"Did Bertie ever tell you why he broke off our engagement? He told me… he said he loved me but that he wasn't right for me, that I should find someone who wouldn't break my heart. Did…"

Her voice faded out, dropping her question, unfinished. Georgie picked it up for her. "Did he meet someone else? No. I would have known. Good Lord, the whole of Yorkshire would have known if Bertie had a girl. Absolutely not."

Ellie smiled weakly.

"I'm afraid I can't help you. Bertie loved to talk about absolutely anything but himself. Or at least anything serious about himself. I suppose his family – well, I'm sure you knew – they were very much against the match. Particularly his mother in that regard, and…"

"And…?" Ellie raised an eyebrow as Georgie's voice trailed off. "And Richard?"

Georgie stood suddenly, picking up the decanter again only to find it empty. "Gosh, we seem to have run out. Perhaps I should fetch another?"

Ellie stood too. "No, that's quite alright. I'm not really in the mood for drinking. I should go and see how things are with everything that has happened. It's probably not the time, but I will need to know how I might get back to Southampton."

Georgie's face fell, shaking off the smile it had held since she stepped through the kitchen door. "Oh, that's all for another time. It's been quite the emotional day. Please stay. Perhaps a tea?"

Ellie suddenly stopped and stared through the window to where the doors of Malkie's garage stood open. She could see the car, pushed tight against the wall where she presumed it had been moved when they lifted it in a vain attempt to save Malkie. To the back of it, a blue-black floor jack lay on its side. A dark thought suddenly hit her.

"I should find Richard, see what happened. I have a terrible feeling this may be partly my doing."

Georgie stepped towards her. "My dear, how could this possibly be your fault?"

Ellie blew out her cheeks. "I drove the car very hard yesterday, had to brake hard to slow for the corner at the duck pond. If he was working on the back of the car, he might have been inspecting the brakes. Suppose I damaged them somehow, and that's why—"

"Nonsense!" Georgie snapped. "Besides, even if you did, you didn't cause the car to fall on him. It could have happened at any time."

"I need to know," Ellie said. "I'm going to take a look and see what happened."

"Wait for me!" Georgie called as Ellie swept out of the drawing room and through the hall to push open the door to the grounds. As she stepped out onto the gravel, she could see a black police bicycle leant against the frame of one of the grand downstairs windows, but no sign of its rider or Richard. The gravel crackled under her feet as she turned around the side of the east wing and into the collection of stone outbuildings that cloistered the side of the building there. The dark green doors of the garage stood open and she stepped inside.

Malkie's tool box was still open on the floor, a wrench and torch lying on the stone flags where she assumed he'd dropped them in his final moments. She picked up the floor jack, trying its handle to push its circular base against her foot. There was no movement or give in the hydraulics that might indicate a fault. If the jack had given way, it must have not been secured properly, she thought. But if it had slipped, it should still be open in the position where it held the car – and the jack was closed. She propped it against the garage wall, inspecting it again curiously.

Ellie lowered herself onto her back and wriggled her way under the car, Malkie's torch in hand. The space below the axle was tight, even for someone her size, and she could see he would have had to have raised the car quite high in order to fit his heavy frame.

"See anything?"

Ellie instinctively tried to sit up at the sound of Georgie's voice, cursing under her breath as her head hit hard metal. "Not yet. I'm just checking something. It's – oh!"

"What is it?" Georgie said, almost touching her toes as she craned her long, thin neck down to try to see under the car.

Ellie pulled herself out, dusting down the grit and dirt from her back, and touching her head where she could feel a small bruise rising. "It's the brakes alright, but I don't think it was me."

"How do you mean?" Georgie said, her brow furrowing as she helped pick a small piece of oiled fabric from Ellie's hair.

"It looks very much like someone has been playing around with them – they've been opened up on the left side and not put back together properly."

"Perhaps Malkie had just…"

"That's what I thought for a moment," Ellie said, looking around carefully on the floor with the torch, although the garage was brightly lit by the overhead sun now. "But it seems like someone has stripped away the brake lining, and there's no sign of any of it here."

"Why on earth would someone do that?" Georgie said, lowering her finely-sculpted eyebrows.

Ellie scratched her head, catching more of the grit it had picked up from the floor in her fingers and flicking it away. "I don't know. Perhaps they were hoping to cause an accident on the road? Or perhaps…" She looked down again at the car jack.

"Perhaps what?" Georgia implored.

"Perhaps someone wanted Malkie to be under the car this morning. Perhaps this wasn't an accident after all."

CHAPTER 7

"SO, run this all past me again. So I can be absolutely sure about this." Georgie was pacing the floor of the drawing room so much Ellie thought she might wear right through what was left of the fading weave of the old carpet.

"Well, the way I see it is this," Ellie said, putting her hands together at her chin. "The jack was in perfect condition and if Malkie was under the car fixing the brakes there's no way he could have reached a jack that was propping the side of the car to accidentally knock it. And it was closed, so someone would have had to close it."

Georgie stopped pacing for a second to fix Ellie with a hard stare. "And you think he was only under the car because someone fiddled with the brakes?"

Ellie nodded. "That would seem the most likely explanation."

Georgie waved her arm theatrically. "But not the only one. Malkie might have taken the... boot–"

"Shoe. Brake shoe."

"Boot, shoe, yes, whatever footwear you like – he might have taken it apart himself and put the bits somewhere?"

Ellie shrugged. "Possibly, but–"

"Now you see," Georgie said sharply, "I can't be doing with 'possiblys'. Possiblys are what will get me laughed out of court before I even get the chance to get into it. I need 'certainlys' if we are about to start accusing people of... well you know what."

Georgie's expression backed up the seriousness of her words, and told Ellie she might need to slow down. They had been going over what they saw in the garage for well over an hour now, while they waited for Richard to return from wherever he had gone with the police officer. Georgie had explained to Ellie her ambitions to be England's first female barrister. She was currently waiting to hear about her standing at the Inns of Court, who she explained were the gatekeepers to a profession that had been barred for women until little more than a year before. Ellie certainly didn't want to drag her into anything that might spoil her reputation before she had the chance to prove herself – and it seemed there were plenty in the Inns who would like nothing more than to see an upstart woman embarrass herself with wild claims of murder.

"Of course," Ellie said. "I'm just exploring the possibilities. I feel I should say something to the police, I just–"

"Just don't go accusing anyone of bumping him off. Not just yet. Please." Georgie's voice had gone from stern instruction to gentle pleading, and Ellie acknowledged it with a nod.

"No, I won't do that. But let's just say someone did 'bump him off'–"

Georgie raised her eyebrows. "Very well, let's just say that. You say they would need to know about cars?"

"Yes. They certainly knew exactly what to do to get Malkie in the right place under the car. And how to do it."

"Well," Georgie said, "that rules out pretty much anyone here. Bertie was the only car lover in the family – spent hours in that garage tinkering with this and that. Half the time you saw him he was covered in oil or grease. Richard – now he wouldn't know one end of a car from another. No interest in them at all, except to get from one place to another. I doubt he even knows how to fill the petrol tank."

Ellie shrugged. "What about that man who brought in the game for Mrs Madison?"

"Jim? Well, yes, I suppose he might know a thing or two. He drove a bit in the army I believe. But he's hardly the cold-eyed killer type, he gets spooked shooting a bunny rabbit. Then there's Mrs Madison, well that's ridiculous – Mr Madison probably knows more about cars than she does. And Lucy, she's barely able to change a light-bulb, I shouldn't imagine she knows the first thing about brakes and whatnot. No – I really can't see anyone here who might know what to do, even if they wanted to do it. And why anyone here would want to, I have no idea."

"Did Malkie have any enemies?" Ellie asked.

"Enemies?" Georgie leant back against the table, half-sitting as she rubbed her angular chin. "Well, he could be a cantankerous old so-and-so at times, but I can't imagine he'd do anything that would see someone want to drop an automobile on him. Poor chap."

Ellie leaned forward, glancing towards the door before she spoke. "Well, I did wonder. I heard something in the car that…" She stopped, suddenly aware of how she might sound. "No, don't worry. Ignore me."

Georgie tilted her head, her interest clearly piqued. "In the car? With Richard?"

"Well yes," she said, leaning forward once more, a little further this time. "But I'm sure it was nothing. The two of them were… well, it was a bit frosty. Malkie seemed to think old Lord Melmersby had given him something, and that Richard knew about it. He sounded quite unhappy about it."

"Gosh!" Georgie exclaimed, standing suddenly from the table. "Well that does sound dreadfully cloak-and-dagger. Is that the term I'm looking for? Hold on, no – I mean utterly barmy! Dear Richard would not hurt a fly. Now this is all very exciting but perhaps we should wait to see what the police say before we go accusing the new Lord Melmersby, and a very old friend of mine, of murdering his chauffeur."

Georgie said the words with a tone of good-humoured scolding, but Ellie knew she was probably right. This could wait for the police, she was a guest here – and not the most welcome one at that – and it wouldn't do to start pointing any fingers. Not yet, anyway, she thought.

Had she wanted to, it now appeared the perfect opportunity had presented itself. No sooner had they agreed to let the talk of murder in the garage drop, than they heard the sound of footsteps on the gravel and the front door opening. Ellie stood up as the drawing room door slowly swung open and Richard walked in, closely followed by a policeman, whose round, flat face and just-too-far-apart eyes had a look that made her imagine a permanently startled French Bulldog.

"Georgie, how lovely to see you. You've met our guest I see. Terrible business with poor Malkie. I do hope you are alright. This is PC Wade." Richard spoke each sentence in a quick staccato, as if he couldn't get the pleasantries over with quickly enough. Georgie hugged him enthusiastically, and kissed him once each cheek; something he accepted with just enough grace so as not to appear rude.

"We've been over all the details of the accident, getting all the paperwork and whatnot in place," Richard continued. "Poor Lucy was a bit shaken with what happened, so she asked for the rest of the week off and I've given her a little extra in her pay packet to recuperate at Harrogate Spa."

"Are you here to ask us about Malkie?" Georgie said to the police officer, her voice a little tighter than before and her eyes darting to Ellie quickly.

"No ma'am," PC Wade said in a broad, deep Yorkshire accent. "That's all in t' hands of t' coroner now. I'm here on t'other matter."

"He's here about the break-in," Richard put in. "Seems there's been some development. He asked to see the damage to the window and so on, for the court records."

"You've caught someone?" The tone of genuine surprise in Georgie's voice made Ellie think that the local police actually catching someone might be something of a rarity.

"Aye ma'am. Young Tom Rabbit. Caught him red-handed last night. Guilty as you like."

"I rather think that's the place of the courts to decide," Georgie snapped, and PC Wade's face looked even more startled than before.

"Seems he was trying to pay off a few bar debts with my silver cup," Richard said.

"Claims as he found it," PC Wade said, his voice rising sharply. "Found it while runnin' a line for crayfish under old Melmersby Beck bridge. If you believe that, you'll believe anything."

"Do you believe that, Richard?" Georgie said, ignoring the snorts that accompanied PC Wade's vigorous head-shaking.

He paused for a second. "I'm not sure. Tom's an honest lad, and not the sort I would imagine could get in and out of a house without being noticed. Well, the fact he was trying to pay for beer with a rather distinctive stolen silver cup should tell you enough about how sharp he is. I mean to speak to him after we've all got tomorrow out of the way."

"Tomorrow?" Ellie asked, looking at Georgie for a prompt.

Richard glared darkly at her. "Yes, tomorrow. My father's memorial service. You do recall why you are here, I hope?"

Ellie blushed. Her head was still in the garage, with the faultless jack and the tampered brakes. How could she forget? "I'm so sorry – it's been such a whirlwind, I forgot what day it is."

Georgie put her arm sympathetically to Ellie's shoulder and Richard's face softened as he spoke more calmly. "Of course, I suppose it has been quite a distracting time. I apologise."

Ellie nodded to show she accepted and Georgie clapped her hands to snap away the clouds that seemed to have descended on the room.

"Right!" she said. "Richard, you should take the constable here to see the damage – I am taking Ellie out for a walk and some fresh air and sunshine. Tomorrow is going to be a dark enough day, we should get some light while we can."

"Aye," PC Wade said. "Well the village has had more than its share of dark days of late, right enough."

"Exactly," Georgie said. "And let's just hope we don't see any more for a good while now."

CHAPTER 8

RICHARD Lindley's father may well have held the ancient title of Melmersby, and been lord of all he surveyed, Ellie thought, but he was living – or should that be dead – proof that money and power can't always buy you true friends.

"Is this everyone?" she whispered to Georgie, who was busily straightening out the collar of her white blouse for her as Ellie inspected the sombre black dress Lucy had picked out in the gold-framed mirror that hung on the far wall of the entrance hall.

Georgie looked around again at the small gathering: Richard; Mrs Madison; a well-dressed couple whose names Ellie had already forgotten; Jim Turnbull and his pinch-faced, grey-haired mother; and Dr Waterman, a childhood friend of Richard's. "That's everyone," she said.

"Ah, you must be Bertie's American fillie? So the old boy wasn't fibbing when he said he'd bagged himself a Yankee beauty." The male half of the couple whose names she had forgotten had pushed his way through the small gathering to place himself right where Ellie and Georgie stood, putting out his hand in greeting.

"Ah, Archie, absolutely, this is Ellie. Ellie—" Georgie held out her downturned palm towards the man, "this is Archie Beauclère, please be prepared to believe every story you hear about him."

Archie beamed, his open hand still outstretched to take Ellie's. "I shall make sure you only hear the good ones."

"And I am his wife, Vivienne." A tall, elegantly dressed woman nipped quickly into the gap, thrusting her hand between Archie and Ellie to take hers in a handshake. "Sorry, but if I leave it to him to introduce me you shan't get my name until next Christmas." She glared at her husband, then offered a forced smile to Ellie. She had a striking beauty about her, Ellie thought, albeit one tempered by how tired she looked.

"Good to meet you, Vivienne," Ellie said, offering a more genuine smile back. "And you too, Archie. I hear you were friends with Lord Melmersby."

"My family has known theirs for many years," Vivienne said. "We Summervilles are the oldest family in this part of Yorkshire, whatever claim you might hear from the Lindleys, and we have ties with each other going back generations. So many of us have married one another over the years we're practically the same family now."

"I just know them through Vivienne," Archie said with a shrug. "I'm afraid I don't come from such illustrious circles; self-made man and all that. But Richard and Bertie were good sorts, and old Lord Melmersby was a fine, upstanding sort of chap."

"Yes," Vivienne said, turning from her husband and looking to Ellie as if she might have caught a whiff of something Mr Madison had left. "My family name has opened a lot of doors for people who would never have got through them without it. Well I suppose I should let you hurry along, the carriages leave shortly and you will wish to be properly dressed by then I'm sure."

Ellie looked at the dress she was wearing and back to the mirror, unsure how to respond.

"Oh, I'm terribly sorry," Vivienne said, inspecting the dress again with a look of what Ellie thought might be pity. "You are wearing this to the service?"

"Lucy picked this out for me," Ellie said, trying to appear unruffled. "I think it's kind of elegant."

"I see." She drawled the second word out as she ran her eyes up and down Ellie again. "A servant girl's choice for an American. I suppose it would seem elegant in that case. Well, it suits you well enough. Come, Archie! Lovely to meet you, Emily, and I am sure we shall speak again."

"It's Ellie, not…"

Archie shrugged and grinned apologetically as his wife strode, straight-backed, to rejoin the others in the small gathering. "I'm afraid Vivienne is very much a Yorkshire lass," he said. "She speaks her mind, but she's a good egg really. Can I offer you a cigarette?"

Ellie shook her head with as graceful a smile as she could manage.

"Do you mind if I do?" he asked, pulling out a silver cigarette case before anyone had time to answer, then flicking in frustration at a matching silver lighter. "Well dash it, I forgot to fill her again. Excuse me, will you."

Archie fumbled in his jacket pocket to pull out a paper book of matches and lit his cigarette to draw a long, relieved smoke. Ellie glanced at the image on the front of the book, a gilded crown held by two upright stags. It struck her that, whether the door had been opened to him by his wife or not, Archie, like all the others here, belonged to that set who have their own coat of arms on their disposables, and she began to feel further from home than she had since she first got off the ship in Southampton

"Oh just ignore her," Georgie said as Archie slunk away to rejoin his wife among the huddled mourners. "Terrible snob, but then her family are absolutely loaded, so she can afford to be."

Ellie turned her head to inspect her dress again. She wasn't one for dresses, or black for that matter, but it appeared a fine one to her. She was relieved that Lucy was still away on her convalescent break so she didn't have to hear her taste questioned in such a rude way.

"Her husband seemed nice enough, though," she said, finally deciding she was perfectly happy with her clothes.

"Well, nice is one word for it," Georgie said, raising a single, finely-drawn eyebrow. "Charming is another. An absolute cad might be the most apposite word."

"Cad?"

"Bounder. Rake. N'er-do-well. Playboy. Terribly good company, and always fun to have around – unless you are some pretty lady's husband, or Archie's wife. He's the sort of fellow who sees marriage vows as optional guidelines, if you know what I mean. It's little wonder she's such a sourpuss."

Ellie looked back over to the couple to see Vivienne now bending the ear of the vicar and Archie casually straightening his waxed moustache by the reflection of a well-polished armour breastplate mounted to the wall of the entrance hall. "If it's that bad, why don't they divorce?"

"Oh that would never happen," Georgie declared. "Poor Vivienne; despite everything, she remains madly in love with him, and besides, her faith would not allow it. As for Archie, well he doesn't have two brass farthings of his own to rub together. He relies totally on her family's money. The man simply can't afford to be without her."

Ellie looked again at Vivienne, this time with a more sympathetic eye. She may have lost the man she thought she would marry, but for some people, it seemed, that might have been an easier heartbreak. Her melancholy thoughts were broken by the sound of Richard's voice.

"Miss Blaine?"

"Oh sorry, I was miles away." She lifted her head and put on a smile.

"I do wonder if you would care to join me, ahead of the ceremony? I am taking the first carriage, to make sure everything is in place before we begin. I thought it might be a chance for you to have a quiet moment. You know, with Bertie."

Ellie's head instantly cleared itself of any other thoughts and she shook herself back into the room. "That's very kind of you, Dr Lindley. Thank you. That would be wonderful."

Georgie gripped her friend's hand and silently mouthed the words to ask if she was alright. Ellie could feel the water rising in her eyes, and dabbed at them with the back of a gloved hand, nodding at Georgie. "I'm fine, thank you."

* * *

The carriage ride was a short one. The small church was set within the grounds of the hall, and served only the Lindley family and their household. But it was long enough that Ellie could finally ask Richard some of the questions that had troubled her since the moment that first, terrible telegram arrived.

"What happened to Bertie, Richard? I mean – I know what happened, but you say you were there; could you maybe let me know? I'd like to know."

Richard lifted his head stiffly, keeping his eyes fixed ahead on the narrow, rutted road that led by the side of a small woodland. "I shouldn't tell you everything. It was a bloody affair, the whole war. Bertie's last day was no different."

"You told me, in the telegram, he died a hero. Was that right?"

Richard's face betrayed no emotion, but he turned now to look at her. "It was at place called Lekkerboterbeek, a small creek the army was determined to cross, without regard to cost it seems. It was madness. They sent them over the top knowing damn well there was no chance. Bertie, of course, was first to go over. He never seemed to care for himself, but he was determined to get his men through if he could. It was hopeless though; they were cut down before they even made it twenty yards. Even the fools who sent them over could see the folly and called them back.

"Well, Bertie made it back into the trench. But not all his boys did. A dozen were down, and four of them wounded and trapped out there in No-Man's Land. The damn fool didn't listen, he went straight back over the top. Bought three of them back, but his luck ran out on the fourth. Caught a shot from a German sniper just as he was leaving the trench again, and that was it. I was with him, you know. When it happened, when he...."

Richard's voice trailed away, betraying the emotion his face still refused to show. For a moment Ellie felt the urge to put her hand to his where it held the reins of the single black horse that pulled their carriage. She held it back, sure he would not welcome any show of that kind now.

"Here we go," Richard said, any trace of emotion now firmly removed from his voice. "It's not much to look at, but it's rather full of history."

The road had turned round to the back of the woods to reveal a small, stone church – not much bigger than the outbuilding that had been turned into Malkie's garage. A short, rather stumpy steeple, faced with an ancient-looking sundial, stood out above an arched entrance. All around, the grey stone of graves, ancient and more modern, dotted the rich grass. Ellie gulped slightly at the site of a freshly dug plot, the dark soil piled to the side of the hollow that awaited a new occupant.

"That's for Malkie," Richard said calmly, seeing where Ellie's eyes had landed. "Father has already been laid to rest within the church. That's where Bertie is too. Whoa!" He pulled tight on the rein, turning the horse's head to one side to bring the carriage to a halt before stepping down briskly and offering his arm to help Ellie out.

"I shall wait outside," he said. "You will see Bertie's marker to the left of the font, set into the wall. I shall give you some time alone with him."

"Thank you," Ellie said. "You are very kind."

"Not at all," Richard said flatly. "I just know he would have wanted you to have the chance to say goodbye. The others will be here in about ten minutes, so…" He gestured towards the open door of the church, and she smiled sadly.

Ellie walked past the low iron railings that guarded the entrance to the church. To the side, a clutch of wild daffodils, a little late in blooming in the shadow of the porch, danced gently in the breeze. Beside them, just where the sunlight dappled the waving grass, a single blue cornflower broke the ground – already shedding the first of its delicate petals. Ellie leant over to pick the simple bouquet, and clutched it to her chest as she stepped into the darkness of the doorway.

ELLIE BLAINE 1920s MYSTERIES

CHAPTER 9

THE Beauclères were the first to break the silence of the dimly lit church, bickering as they jostled each other through the door. Ellie smiled politely at them and they broke off from their squabble just long enough to nod acknowledgement back. Richard came in behind them, quickly followed by the rest of the small throng of mourners.

The vicar arrived last: a short, plump and slightly breathless figure, with an air of self-importance that felt disproportionate to the size of his church.

He walked between the pews to take his place at the front, quickly glancing around the congregation for a moment before a forced, headmasterly, cough brought everyone's attention to his round, bespectacled head rising just above the oversized pulpit.

Ellie looked around, at the monuments and memorials, the vicar's dry, monotonous voice drifting in and out of her hearing as she read the history of the Lindley family in stone. To her left, she saw another Richard; gone so long his epitaph was in Latin, which she could read only enough of to see he'd died in 1621: almost 300 years to the day. She imagined someone just like her, sitting here all those years ago and remembering that Richard the same way she now remembered Bertie – and of someone 300 years from now reading Bertie's name in this place and knowing as little of him as she did of his long-gone ancestor.

The congregation stood, bringing Ellie sharply back from her thoughts, and she followed them up, hastily scrambling in her hymn book while looking over Archie Beauclère's shoulder in front of her to find the proper page. The mourners fidgeted their way through a few verses, badly sung by most, with only Richard's deep baritone and the surprisingly sweet mezzo-soprano of Mrs Madison giving Ellie any sort of clue as to what melody she should be singing. A final prayer was read for the soul of Lord Melmersby while Mrs Madison dabbed her eyes, and the vicar stepped down to speak condolences to Richard and then the rest of the throng as they made their way out of the church.

Outside in the light, the vicar's air of serious self-importance seemed to melt into a jollier form of pomposity, as he chatted loudly about how old Lord Melmersby was always so generous to the church, and how much it might cost to replace his old vestments which had been got at by moths.

Ellie politely broke away from the renewed attentions of Archie, who was trying to persuade her to go for a spin in his new two-seater, and joined Georgie, who was standing alone just outside the church porch.

"Everything alright, darling?" Georgie asked, taking hold of Ellie's hand. "Did you get to say your goodbyes?"

She nodded, shaping a smile as well as she could. "I did, thank you. I–"

"Ah, Georgina. Now there's a face I haven't seen on a Sunday for quite a while." The vicar's pudding face broke into a deep smile as he grabbed one of Georgie's hands firmly between both of his. His voice managed to be simultaneously cheery and admonishing in almost exact equal measure, Ellie thought.

"Rev Barton, what a lovely sermon you gave," Georgie replied convincingly. "Lord Melmersby would have been most grateful I am sure."

The vicar swatted away the praise less convincingly, insisting he was a poor speaker to eulogise such a fine man. "It would not become a man of my station to sing his own praises, and Heaven knows I am no great orator, but the late Lord Melmersby did enjoy my sermons, I know that much. He told me himself he only ever wanted me for weddings, baptisms and funerals as to hear me every Sunday would be like caviar every breakfast time – too much of such a luxury would reduce it to the commonplace."

"Oh, absolutely Rev Barton, we shouldn't want to spoil ourselves so much on such rich fare," Georgie said, with what Ellie thought was an impressively straight face.

"And on the subject of such special days," the vicar continued, "we do all still wonder when you might take a little trip to Melmersby parish church with a certain gentleman?"

Ellie looked at Georgie, who subtly raised her eyes and shook her head. "I'm afraid there is no 'certain gentleman' at the moment, vicar. When there is, you shall be the first to know."

Rev Barton raised his hands in mock-surrender. "You are quite the tricky fish to catch, I think, Miss Parr." He held the word 'Miss' just long enough for it to be a hiss. "Perhaps your friend here could find an able sportsman to reel you in, hey?"

Georgie stepped back a little, to put her friend to the fore. "Of course, how rude of me. Ellie, this is the Reverend John Barton. And Reverend, this is Ellie Blaine."

The vicar took as deep a bow as his belly would allow, and Ellie dropped her head in return. "Delighted to make your acquaintance, Miss Blaine. It is 'Miss' is it?"

"The Reverend is always keen to learn the status of any young women in his parish in regards to matrimony," Georgie said with a disarming smile. "Especially those whose fathers are in a position to spare no expense on their daughter's wedding day."

Ellie laughed silently. The vicar would definitely have no interest in her prospects then, she thought.

"We all rather hoped Miss Parr might tie the knot with poor young Bertram Lindley, of course," the vicar said. "That would have been the wedding of the decade."

Georgie looked urgently at Ellie shaking her head. "I think some people may have misunderstood the nature of our friendship in that regard, Rev Barton. We were fine friends, and nothing more."

The vicar grunted what seemed like acceptance of this fact. "Well, as you say. I suspect we were all just hoping you might be the one to save us all from his absurd plan to marry some dreadful American sales girl. Thank the Lord he saw sense there in the end. Can you imagine?"

Georgie's mouth turned to an awkward grimace as Ellie smiled disarmingly back at the vicar, then spoke in her deepest Indiana accent. "Well, it's been mighty nice to meet you, sir, and if you ever find yourself out in the beautiful city of Indianapolis, be sure to pop in to Ernie Drammer' car salesroom, where I shall do my best to make you feel as welcome as you've been kind enough to make me feel here."

Rev Barton's fleshy face turned a deep purple as he spluttered. "Oh! Of course, I didn't mean… I was simply… it's just…"

Ellie and Georgie turned sharply to walk away, leaving the vicar to stammer apologies after them. Georgie linked her arm through Ellie's and they looked at each other for a moment, before doubling over in laughter behind the strategic shelter of a tall memorial obelisk.

"Oh dear, poor Rev Barton. Did you see his face?" Georgie puffed out her cheeks and dropped her voice to match his plummy tone. "Can you imagine? Not just a dreadful sales woman, a dreadful American sales woman. It would be the end of Melmersby, the end of Yorkshire, the end of England!"

Ellie wiped away a tear of laughter. For the first time since she'd arrived in Melmersby, she suddenly felt like it matched the place Bertie had told her about, or at least how she'd imagined it – the good and the bad.

"We should get back," Georgie said, gathering her breath again. "The carriages are leaving." She nodded over to where Richard was waiting beside the two-wheel carriage that had brought them there, the first of the other carriages already turning around the edge of the wood back towards the house.

"I think I might just stay here a short while," Ellie said. "I wanted to have a look around. Bertie told me so much about the wood and the river back here, I thought I might spend a little time alone, you know, in the places he talked about."

Georgie nodded. "I shall tell Richard. It's a good half hour walk back to the house. Dinner is at eight – so give yourself plenty of time. Mrs Madison is very particular about starting dinner on time." Georgie mimicked the waving of a rolling pin and Ellie laughed. "You'll need to give yourself time to change for dinner too."

Ellie looked down again at her black dress. The only time she changed for dinner at home was if she needed to get out of her overalls and wash the oil off her hands after working on Old Pepper Pot. She imagined this might take a little longer. She waved off Georgie as Richard shook the reins to gee their horse forward, and Ellie took another look at the church – now empty and quiet again – and whispered a quiet 'goodbye'. She walked down through the thick grass that edged the back of the wood near the church, down to the swift-flowing narrow brook and small wooden bridge that sat in a sunlit clearing at the bottom of a shallow slope. Set back from the river was the cottage where Jim Turnbull and his mother lived; small and neat, the shingle roof softened with moss and the scent of woodsmoke from the red clay chimney pot. She lay down in the warmth of Spring grass and closed her eyes to the buzzing of bees bumbling among the red clover and buttercups, and thought of the stories she had heard about this place when it had all seemed like a dream she would never wake up from.

ELLIE BLAINE 1920s MYSTERIES

CHAPTER 10

SHE woke with a start. An orange-speckled butterfly had landed on her cheek, brushing its soft wings against her face to pull her from a dream of ginger cats chasing her in a car with no steering wheel around hair-pin bends. For a moment she was unsure where she was, then she sat up suddenly as she remembered Georgie's warning about being on time for dinner.

She picked herself up and hurried back up the slope towards the church. The clear skies of earlier had now thickened over with cloud and she had to squint at the old dial on the tower. She could barely make out the shadow on its weather-worn face: was that 6:30, or 7? Ellie shook her head as she fumbled in her bag for her watch to confirm. Damn! 7:30.

For dinner at eight. What did Georgie say? Half an hour back to the house? That's if you walk. Quicker if you run!

Ellie pulled off her narrow, heeled shoes. Lucy had picked a size too large, so they would fall off when she got moving anyway, and the ground was soft between here and the house. She took a deep breath, put her head down, and kicked up her legs.

The house seemed to take forever to come into view, and as long again to reach once it did. When she finally made it to the steps of the entrance hall she was relieved no one seemed to be around to see her muddy feet and dress, sodden from the evening dew, and her face equally soaked in sweat. She quickly and quietly stepped her aching legs up the wide, turning staircase and along the corridor to her room, where she splashed her hot face with water then wriggled her way as neatly as she could from one dress into another which she picked almost at random from the rail.

Giving herself a moment to calm her breath and let the colour disappear from her cheeks, she prepared herself to be ready to descend the stairs and enter the dining room with as much calm grace as she could muster, when there was a hard rap on her bedroom door.

"One second!" she called, pulling the dress free where it had caught itself up in its own ruffles. "Come in!"

She straightened herself, trying her best to look as unflustered as possible, while casually flattening the last stubborn ruffle that still clung, untamed, to the top of her stockings. Richard looked at her with an expression she was annoyed to find she couldn't read.

"Ah, so you are back. Dinner will be a little late. The Beauclères are... taking a moment to themselves," he said. "We shall be dining in half an hour."

The door closed behind him before she could finish a relieved "thank you" and she sat down sharply on the bed, puffing her cheeks out in relief. She imagined, from their demeanour as they left church together, that the Beauclère's 'moment' might be the source of the shouting she could now hear faintly echoing down the corridor from somewhere in the sprawling building. She lay back on the bed, pushing the soft, plump pillow around her head, and closed her eyes.

When the knock came again to finally go down to dinner, she was feeling a lot more composed, and a lot hungrier. She was pleased to see Mrs Madison had decided not to stand on ceremony and their soup bowls were already full with what smelt like a particularly good chowder. Ellie had been given a place between Georgie and the man she'd been told was Richard's old friend, Dr Simon Waterman. He introduced himself with a firm handshake and a boyish grin, and Ellie was relieved to see that he, at least, appeared friendly and welcoming.

The atmosphere across the table was considerably less convivial. It seemed that, while the

Beauclères had calmed down enough to be able to dine together, whatever quarrel they had was far from over. Vivienne was silently washing down nearly every mouthful she ate with a good gulp of wine and refilling her glass as quickly as it emptied. Archie, meanwhile, was ignoring her completely to restart his boasts about his new car.

"I mean, you would love it, Ellie. She goes like the wind, a real tiger to handle – if you know what I mean. I like that and I suspect you might be the sort of girl to appreciate it too. How about I take you out in her some time and show you exactly what she can do?"

"That's very kind of you," Ellie said as delicately as she could. "But I'm not sure I shall be staying here much longer. I'm sure Vivienne would love a spin in it."

Vivienne looked up from her wine glass and let out a sharp laugh. "Oh, trust me, it's been a long time since Archie wanted to take me out for a spin."

Archie grinned nervously. "Now darling, we are at dinner–"

"Not that I'm complaining," she continued, jabbing a finger at him. "You were never much of a driver, were you?"

"Now dear–"

"No! You were never much of anything, really. It's not even your car. Did he tell you that, Ellie? It's not even his car."

Dr Waterman sat up straight, trying as best he could to quickly move the conversation on to somewhere more convivial. "Now chaps, I'm not sure this is the place. It's been quite a trying day. I hear you both just got back yesterday from a few days in London. How is the old place?"

Vivienne appeared in no mood to change the subject. "It's not even your car, is it? You don't actually own anything do you, you just take, take, take. And all I do is give, and I am fed up of it. I am…" Vivienne's words slurred to a halt and she stopped to stare into her empty glass.

"I'm not sure you are looking too well, Vivienne," Dr Waterman said, standing fully now to move towards where she was leaning back a little precariously in her chair. "Perhaps you'd like a spot of fresh air?"

"I am so sorry," Archie said, looking around the table. "She started drinking before the service, I tried to ask her to slow down. She's really not herself when she's had too much."

"Oh, I'm not myself am I?" Vivienne slurred, pulling her arm away from where Dr Waterman had taken it in a gentle hold. "And who am I? The drunken wife who doesn't understand poor Archie? Is that what you tell her? That little floosie of yours? You think I don't know what you get up to on your so-called 'business trips' – the ones you pay for with my money."

"Darling–"

"Don't you darling me!" Vivienne snapped. "Yes, why don't I tell everyone what sort of a man you are? They will find out soon enough, because I swear I have had more than enough and I will not stand for it any more, I tell you I will not stand for it!"

Ellie watched Vivienne grab at the table to support herself, and wondered whether she might actually be able to stand at all right now. Archie grinned awkwardly across the table at her and Ellie shook her head with an expression that quickly turned his eyes elsewhere.

Vivienne mumbled something again towards Archie, but if anyone could make out the words no one was saying what they were.

"Come on Vivienne old pal," Dr Waterman said, "let's get you somewhere to lie down for a while, you're not feeling too bright are you? It'll be ok, you maybe need a little rest."

"Take her through to the drawing room," Richard said, standing up. "And Mrs Madison, be so good as to cover the chaise longue with some sackcloth from the kitchen and we'll put her to rest there for a while."

Richard draped Vivienne's arm over his shoulder and put his arm around her back, Dr Waterman supporting her from the other side as they lifted her up out of her chair.

"Thank you," Vivienne said. Then louder as if to the whole room. "Thank you, Richard. You were always such a gentleman. Always such a gentleman!"

"That's quite alright, Vivienne," Richard said, smiling awkwardly. "Let's just get you settled–"

"I should have married you when I had the chance, Richard. I should have. I was such a fool, wasn't I?"

Richard's face coloured slightly and he heaved a stumbling Vivienne further upright. "Come on, Viv, you need to rest. Do you have her Simon?"

Dr Waterman nodded and the two men quickly carried her through to the small anteroom that stood just off the drawing room. "If we leave the door open between here and the drawing room we can hear if she gets in a worse way," Dr Waterman said as he and Richard returned. "Is that alright, Archie? You can go and sit with her if you think it would help."

Archie shook his head. "I think maybe it would be better if she has a little time to herself," he said sheepishly.

The table was silent for a while, before Mrs Madison returned to place a heavy dish of game pie down with a thump that woke up the atmosphere.

"That smells absolutely delicious, Mrs Madison," Georgie said.

"Well, it's nothing fancy," Mrs Madison said brusquely. "There's only me in the kitchen today, so I do my best. That's all I can do, what with the cleaning, and the waiting table and what not. I just do my best." She turned deliberately and marched back to the kitchen to bring the rest of the trimmings.

"Your father certainly ran a tight ship here at the end, didn't he?" Simon smiled. "Poor Mrs Madison. What happened to the rest of the staff?"

Richard shook his head. "Father had a way of falling out with people, as you know. Towards the end he fell out with them more quickly than he could replace them."

"Perhaps word got round that the place was practically empty?" Georgie said. "You really should have someone here to look after the place, what with the break-in."

Dr Waterman looked up from his plate. "You had a break-in? Sorry to hear that, Richard. There seems to be a lot of that about. Had someone come through the window at my surgery about six months back – wouldn't be surprised if it's the same lot."

"Oh dear," Georgie said. "Did they take much?"

Dr Waterman shook his head. "Not as far as I can see. Made a right mess of my office though. Not much in there worth the bother of breaking in, I don't think, unless you want to pinch some paperclips. I did wonder if they were looking for laudanum or such like; you know the kind, Richard. Of course I don't keep anything like that in my surgery, but I wouldn't expect that kind of person to know that."

"You're the local doctor here, Simon?" Ellie asked.

"I am, yes," he said with a smile. "I cover most of the villages around here, got my little surgery down Sidthorpe way, just over the back of those hills you can see from the lawn."

"Simon and I trained together," Richard said. "He was quite the most brilliant student among us all. You won't find a better doctor from here to Harley Street."

Dr Waterman blushed. "Oh come on Richard! You know that isn't true. You're the one the great and good of London go to when they're feeling poorly. We are all quite jealous of you."

Richard smiled. "You know as well as I do that's only because you care about your community more than chasing the bright lights. You are a far better doctor than I will ever be, and I won't hear another word to the contrary."

Ellie thought she could see Dr Waterman's eyes glisten at Richard's words. For a moment he was silent, then he took up his glass of wine and drank deeply.

"That is far too kind of you, Richard." He paused. "Richard, I just wanted to say, I really appreciate you inviting me here today, after everything. I just want you to know – what I did back then; it was all just a foolish–"

Richard held up his hand. "There's no need, Simon. It is long forgotten."

Dr Waterman dropped his head. "I'm sorry. That's all I wanted to say. I'm so deeply sorry."

Ellie looked at Georgie, who shook her head, looking as confused as she felt.

"Perhaps we should move to the drawing room?" Richard said suddenly, raising himself up in his chair as if to stand. "We've dined splendidly and

I should like to stretch out a little before we retire for the night. Simon, perhaps you would like an after-dinner cigar?"

"That would be delightful." Simon smiled.

"It would," Archie said keenly.

Richard held Archie's gaze for a moment, then gestured with his hand to move him through to the withdrawing room. "I'm afraid they may be a little old," he said. "They were father's. It's not a habit I indulge in myself."

Mrs Madison, who had just entered the room to begin clearing dishes, looked flustered. "Will you be needing anything bringing through? It's just I've got all this—"

"Don't worry, Mrs Madison, Lucy is back in the morning. Leave the clearing up until then and go and get yourself an early night."

"Well that is kind of you, sir" she said. "But if I leave this place a mess the mice will get in and—"

"Mr Madison can take care of those," Richard said. "Off you go to get some rest, you've earned it. That's an order!"

The housekeeper muttered some words that might have been thanks under her breath as she took off her apron and disappeared back into the kitchen. The guests walked through to the drawing room and took their places in the mismatched chairs and sofas that took up the best part of the room.

"I should probably go and check on Vivienne," Archie said sheepishly.

"See if she needs any water," Richard said. "I imagine she will have quite the headache in the morning. I shall put some aspirin by for her."

"So," Georgie said as she settled down into the green leather of an oversized armchair, "What plans does the new Lord Melmersby have for this old place? You always said you wanted rid of it, Richard. It would be a shame though, it's been–"

"Richard! Simon! In the name of God, someone come and help!" Archie's face was flushed white as he rushed back into the room.

"What on earth is it, man?" Richard said. The faces of those around him echoed his concern.

"It's Vivienne. I can't wake her. I think… oh Lord, I think she's dead!"

Richard and Simon rushed through to the anteroom, followed quickly by the other guests. Richard held her hand as he pressed his fingers against her wrist, then again on her neck.

"Are you getting anything?" Simon said.

"No pulse," Richard said grimly. "I'm not getting a heartbeat." He put his hand to her forehead then shook his head. "Barely any temperature at all. I'm so sorry, Archie," he said. "I think she must have slipped away while we were dining."

Archie fell to his knees at his wife's side, grasping her hand and lowering his head to sob deeply into her chest.

"My darling, I'm so sorry. I'm sorry for everything. I should have been with you. I should have been a better husband. This is all my fault!" He took her cold hand in his, linking his fingers with hers, then suddenly pulled back, as if in shock. "What the devil is this?" he said, looking around at the baffled faces around him.

Ellie looked down to see his shaking hand held out toward them, palm turned upwards. In it, he cradled a single, tattered white feather.

CHAPTER 11

"RIGHT, so let me get this straight." The detective inspector was pacing the room, pausing just long enough between sentences to try to catch someone's new expression before continuing. "There were six people in the house last night when Mrs Beauclère met her untimely end."

He checked his notebook again, carefully reading out the names, although they'd gone over this several times already, and Ellie was pretty sure DI Lochner knew everyone here personally, apart from her.

"Mr Archibald Beauclère, husband of the deceased…"

Archie, his eyes ringed with red and his face deathly pale, bowed his head.

"Lord Melmersby; Dr Simon Waterman; Miss Hilda Madison…"

Mrs Madison reddened deeply.

"Miss Georgina Parr and Miss Eleanor Blaine."

"That is correct, Carl," Richard said sternly. "I think we established that some while ago."

DI Lochner held Richard's gaze for a moment, before continuing, unruffled. "And a number of the same were in attendance at the house on the morning of Malkie Fawthrop's death?"

"Again," Richard growled. "We have told you that."

"Along with Miss Lucy Madison here, and one Jim Turnbull, not currently present."

DI Lochner was a short, angular man with an impressively sharp nose. Dressed in tweed, Ellie thought he would only need a deerstalker hat to make quite a convincing impression of Sherlock Holmes, something she thought might not be entirely accidental.

"And both Mr Fawthrop and Mrs Beauclère had a feather on their person when they were found," he continued. "We now have reason to believe," he turned to catch Ellie's expression in this pause, "that Mr Malkie's untimely demise was not as accidental as was first thought. Which begs the question, did the same person kill both Malkie Fawthrop and Mrs Beauclère? And is that person now sitting in this room?"

DI Lochner turned his gaze quickly in a full circle, looking deliberately at each face in the room.

"It's also entirely possible that both deaths were accidental," Richard said calmly.

"Accidental, you say?" DI Lochner echoed, moving closer to stare even more intently at Richard. He seemed to like staring, Ellie observed, and she wondered if he thought he might ever catch a criminal simply by staring at them. "And how might Mrs Beauclère's death have been accidental?"

"She had an awful lot to drink," Dr Waterman stepped in. "Perhaps–"

"No Simon," Richard said. "It wasn't that. I could smell it on her breath. I know that smell only too well."

"Smell?" the inspector said, staring again.

"Luminal – it's a brand of chloral hydrate. After my brother died it was the only thing that would let my mother sleep. I'd find her passed out on the sofa, her breath smelling the same: of rotten fruit and spirits. She used to keep bottles of the stuff in her little hiding places. I find another one every now and again but I'm sure there are some I've missed. It's quite possible Vivienne found one and thought it to be something else; it can be quite deadly if you take too much. We should wait for the coroner's report, of course, but I can promise you that is what they will find."

"And the feathers? Something of a coincidence in two separate accidents, wouldn't you say?"

Richard shrugged. "Well, it is an odd thing. But there are doves roosting in the garage, and the chaise longue is stuffed with goose down and a little tattered at the seams. I prefer to believe in coincidence rather than that anyone here is a killer."

There were nods and mutterings around the room as the DI once again examined the people sitting there, before turning to Ellie.

"Miss Blaine, you told me a little earlier that you believe that Malkie's car was tampered with prior to his death, and that whoever did it would need to have an intimate knowledge of cars?"

"Well, they would have to know something of how to work on them," Ellie said.

"I see," the inspector said, slowly and deliberately. "Have you heard of a 'Mickey Finn', Miss Blaine."

Ellie frowned, looking instinctively at Richard before responding. "It's something I've read about in true crime stories," she said, puzzled as to where this was going. "It's a drink spiked with something to knock someone out."

"Yes, very good." DI Lochner said. "I am also quite partial to a true crime story, and I happen to know that the 'something' in the drink is that very same chloral hydrate Lord Melmersby believes killed Mrs Beauclère."

"I see," Ellie said, still uncertain why she was now the one being stared at. "So someone gave Vivienne a Mickey Finn?"

"Peculiar, don't you think?" the inspector said, now rising up a little on tiptoe as he spoke. "Two people are dead. One killed by someone with an intimate knowledge of cars, another by a drug used by American gangsters. Both shortly after–"

"Oh come on now!" Georgie stood up suddenly, throwing her arm up in exasperation. "You don't seriously think Ellie did this? What? She comes over from America just to bump off two people she's never even heard of before?"

"I just want to be sure to examine all possibilities," he said, putting his hands to his tweed jacket lapels. "When you have eliminated the impossible, whatever remains, however improbable, must be the truth."

Ellie resisted the urge to laugh.

"Could you tell me exactly where you were between the hours of 7 and 7:30 on the morning of April 3rd."

"Seven and 7:30?" Ellie said, suddenly thinking back.

DI Lochner cleared his throat. "Indeed. We know that Malkie started work at 7am, and that at 7:30am Jim Turnbull called at the garage to enquire about borrowing some oil for his gun, only to get no answer when he knocked. Lord Melmersby also reported, let me see…" The inspector opened up his notebook, wetting a finger to turn its leaves. "Ah, yes, here we are: 'a loud thud, like a heavy object falling'. And this was about 7:10, you said, sir?"

Richard nodded.

"Based on this testimony, and the coroner's report," DI Lochner continued, "We can conclude that Mr Malkie Fawthrop died between 7am and 7:30am on the morning of Sunday April 3rd. So I ask you once again, Miss Blaine, where were you at that time?"

"She was with me." Lucy Madison stood up now. "I brought her breakfast and we had a most pleasant chat. And I hope you don't mind me saying this…" she looked at Richard before continuing. "It's not my place to say but, really, I think it is rather beastly to be questioning a guest in the house in such a way. It's just… not on." Lucy's face flushed and she sat down suddenly, looking at her feet while Mrs Madison scowled at her.

"It is a little unlikely," Richard said. "And I think we have all given a statement as to what happened now, so perhaps we could await the coroner's report and come back to any further questions once you and your team have a little more… clarity in your line of inquiry?"

DI Lochner lifted his chin and breathed in sharply through his nose. "I can assure you, Lord Melmersby, that my team and I shall have many further questions. Of all of you." He looked around the assembled faces one more time then nodded to PC Wade, who had been standing silently by the door the whole time, to signal it was time to go.

"Inspector," Richard said, as he showed the two men to the front door, "I was hoping I might be able to talk to young Tom Rabbit, about the break-in. Would it be convenient to come to the station tomorrow?"

DI Lochner nodded to PC Wade, who passed the nod on to Richard. "Indeed, m' Lord. If you wish."

Richard smiled as he opened the door. "And please, feel free to call in any time if you have further questions."

Mrs Madison and Lucy returned to the kitchens, while Georgie accompanied a pale-faced Archie out to his car. It was mid-afternoon now, and there had been little sleep since the unfortunate events of the previous night.

"I might take a little rest in my room,' Ellie said to Richard as they watched Archie's car disappear down the drive towards the old gatehouse. "Perhaps someone could call me when it is time for dinner?"

Richard nodded. "Indeed, it has been a trying time."

They both turned to go back into the house, to be greeted by Dr Waterman on his way out.

"Ah, Richard. I was hoping to catch you before I left. I wonder, may I have a word with you." He looked at Ellie. "Privately, if I may."

"I was just on my way to my room," Ellie said, smiling politely. "Goodbye, Dr Waterman."

The doctor faintly acknowledged her words with a tip of his head, and Ellie stepped back into the house and made her way up the broad turn of the stairs and along the corridor to her room. She sat down sharply on the bed, puffing out her cheeks and pulling off her shoes; throwing them to the foot of the bed as she dropped backwards into the welcoming softness of pillows and mattress.

"Oh, what a week!" she said out loud to herself. She thought about how glad she would be to get back, to see her mother and her friends again. Even to see the showroom again, to smile and flatter the men who came in to buy cars, to finish a day of work and take a trip to the movies or dance at home to the songs on the radio. Just to be somewhere normal once again, where you didn't have to check under your bed for killers.

"What was that?"

Whatever it was, it was under the bed and she immediately wished her thoughts hadn't gone to that place just at that moment. Carefully, she turned onto her stomach and leaned over the side, lifting the tasselled edges of the bed cover to peer under the gap below her mattress – and at the sight of a fat, ginger cat sat upright, legs wide apart as he licked his great, round belly.

"Mr Madison! What are you doing in here?" she said, turning again to drop her legs over the side of the bed and lower herself down to meet the intruder face-to-face. "Come on, you're not supposed to be in here. Mrs Madison will be looking for you."

Ellie scooped the reluctant cat up into her arms, where he stopped his struggle and draped his wide paws casually over her shoulder, purring loudly in her ear as his whiskers tickled her cheek. Holding his back legs in the crook of one arm, she used the other to open the door. Mr Madison immediately took the chance to jump out of her arms and race away down the corridor in the opposite direction to the entrance hall and the kitchens.

"Mr Madison!" Ellie called back after him. "Come here you crazy cat!"

She wasn't entirely sure why she followed him, he would be sure to know the house a lot better than she did, but she felt a certain amount of responsibility for him being in her room as she had sleepily left her door ajar when she came down to breakfast and the questioning from the police. She caught sight of his ginger bottle-brush tail vanishing around the corner of the corridor that led away from her room and into the older, unused, part of the house. Following after him, she found herself standing on what must once have been the landing of a now boarded-up staircase. The boards were dusty and haphazardly placed so the gaps between them might be wide enough for a cat to fall through. Mr Madison perched precariously at the edge of one of the gaps as Ellie crouched down and softly clicked her tongue to call him.

Suddenly, below her, she heard the sound of a door opening then closing firmly, then voices she recognised immediately as Richard and Dr Waterman. Voices spoken in whispers but with a sense of urgency behind them. She stopped immediately, turning her head to catch their words, a glimpse of the two men standing below through the crack in the boards. Simon nervously fumbled in a cigarette case, offering one to Richard, who shook his head. Dr Waterman lit his up and drew deeply on it.

"Simon, I have told you," Richard said firmly, "you are reading too much into this. I appreciate the situation is a trying one but I'm afraid you are rather letting your imagination run away with you. And besides, I made it clear yesterday it is forgotten. It was years ago. You can't seriously believe—"

"I don't know what to believe," Dr Waterman hissed, in a tone Ellie thought betrayed a sense of fear. "I really don't. Just… talk to me, Richard. Please, if you plan to do anything. We were friends, once."

She heard Richard sigh. "We are friends still, Simon. Perhaps you should go to the police if you believe…"

"You know I won't do that, Richard. I do believe you. I mean, I think I do." Simon let out a bitter laugh. "Well I guess I'll find out won't I. If I'm the next to go. I'll know then."

"Simon. Look; if it was—"

Mr Madison rolled over to better reach his tail with his tongue, and slipped into the gap, wedging his fat, furry back between the floorboards. Ellie instinctively lurched forward to grab him, hauling him back from the precipice by his tail so that he let out a high screech before hissing loudly and scurrying back over the landing floor to disappear the way they had come in. Below them, Richard and Simn had stopped talking to look up at the source of the noise, and Ellie took the cover of Mr

Madison's thundering paws to slip quietly away and back to her room.

ELLIE BLAINE 1920s MYSTERIES

CHAPTER 12

ELLIE didn't go down to dinner that evening. Lucy was sent to call her down, but she made an excuse of tiredness and lack of appetite. There was some truth to both, but caused as much by what she had heard as by the events of the previous night.

Did Simon think Richard killed Malkie and Vivienne? It certainly sounded that way. And he had seemed genuinely concerned that he might be next. And if so, why? What reason would Richard have to kill his chauffeur, an old girlfriend, and possibly his friend from his college years?

Perhaps Simon stole Vivienne from him? That might make revenge a motive, she thought. But then what on earth would old Malkie have to do with that? And what about the quarrel Richard and

Malkie had in the car. Malkie seemed to think Richard had taken something from him – could that something be important enough to kill for?

She stood up suddenly from the chair by the window where she had been resting. Looking out, she could see the door to the garage where Malkie died, still wide open, the place empty now but for dusty workbenches and the rows of tools hanging from the walls. She remembered what the police inspector had said about that morning; that Jim Turnbull had called at the garage at 7:30 only to get no reply. That could mean that, if Richard was around the garage at the time of Malkie's death, Jim might be the only one who would have seen him. If she was going to be stuck here until the investigation concluded, she thought, she might as well make herself useful, and see if she couldn't help conclude it that little bit faster.

She quickly pulled on her old boots and jacket, throwing a shawl Lucy had put out for her across her shoulders for a little extra protection against the cold of the early evening, and slipped down the stairs; tiptoeing across the hall to the exit, being careful not to draw the attention of anyone who might have stepped away from the dinner table. Cautiously, she made her way across the gravel of the driveway and onto the grass that was already wet from evening dew; heading back the way to the church, to the old bridge, and the little cottage where she would find Jim.

***

It was fully dark by the time she passed the old church, and she had to tread carefully down the slope to the little wooden bridge. Now she could see the light from the window of the cottage, flickering as a shadow moved past it. Someone was in, at least.

She knocked firmly on the door, pulling the shawl in closer against the cold as she waited for an answer. Voices came from inside, then the clatter of a chair pulled back and the noise of a rusty bolt turning in its slot, before the door slowly opened a crack to reveal the thin, time-worn face of a woman she recognised from the memorial service.

"Hello!" She smiled nervously. "You must be Jim's mother. I'm Ellie – a friend of Richard's. I'm staying at–"

"I know who you are," the woman said sharply. "What do you want?"

Ellie cleared her throat. "I was just wondering if I might talk with Jim. I just had a couple of questions for him, with regard to what happened… with the accident at the garage."

"Police already asked him," she snapped. "No more questions, he's told them everything he knows."

She went to close the door, when a voice came from behind her. "Who is it, mum?"

"That 'merican woman what was engaged to Bertie," she called back.

"Wha' she want?"

"Talk to you or sum'it."

Ellie grinned sheepishly. She was suddenly not entirely sure why she thought this might be a good idea.

"Let 'er in. I'll talk to 'er," Jim called.

The woman swung the door open and gestured into the house with her head. "He'll talk to yer," she said.

"Thank you," Ellie said, dipping her head to fit under what was a very low doorway and into a clean but sparse and tiny room that made up considerably more than half of the downstairs of the little cottage. Two bowls of steaming soup stood on the table, filling the room with the inviting scent of fresh herbs and roasted vegetables. On the wall behind the table, a shotgun hung next to the bodies of three rabbits and a brace of pigeon.

"Evenin' Miss Blaine," Jim said, touching the brim of a flat cap he had hastily put on as she walked in and stubbing out a thin, hand-rolled cigarette into a faded blue and white saucer. "What c…can I 'elp you with."

"Good evening Jim, thank you," she said, setting herself down on the stool Jim had pulled out for her. He sat down close by on a small wooden chair that put him much lower than her. "I just had a quick question about the morning you called on Malkie, when he had his accident."

"I told you," his mother butted in. "Police already asked all this."

Ellie nodded. "I know Mrs Turnbull, this isn't official or anything, it's just my own curiosity."

Mrs Turnbull huffed and turned her own chair a little to the side to signal she was having no part of any conversation on the matter.

"What is it y…you wanna' know about?" Jim said, trying hard to keep his head up as he talked.

"When you called round for your gun oil, did you see anyone? Anyone in the grounds?"

Jim shook his head. "No, miss. W…windows was all sh…shuttered up like, and lights out on that s…side o' the house. I figured all was still in b…bed miss."

"I 'ope you don't think my Jim had nothin' to do with what 'appened to Malkie and that poor lady," Mrs Turnbull growled, turning her chair back suddenly. "He's a good boy and never did no one no harm."

"No, Mrs Turnbull. Jim wasn't even in the house last night, so no-one thinks he had anything to do with any of that."

"Could have fooled me, way t' police were talkin'," Mrs Turnbull said, shaking her head.

"I din't do nuthin'," Jim said. "Din't see nuthin' neither."

"I know," Ellie said. "Do you know if Malkie or Vivienne had a quarrel with anyone in the Lindley family?"

Mrs Turnbull let out a harsh, sharp laugh. "There's only one man in that family now, if that's what you mean."

Ellie flushed. She didn't want to ask directly if Jim knew of trouble between Richard and the two deceased, but it seemed she had anyway.

"It's not my place to say," Jim said. "'Appen there's always trouble of one k…kind or another in a place like this. I've 'ad my fill of it, I c…can tell you that for nowt. Reckon as I'll be out of here soon enough."

Mrs Turnbull's face softened as she addressed her son. "Now Jim, I told you, you can't be reckonin' on–"

"I told you mum!" Jim's face suddenly darkened and Ellie saw that his upper lip, which already had a slight tic as he spoke, now twitched violently. "I am gettin' out of here and goin' back to t'army. It's where I b…belong. It's where I m…matter."

Mrs Turnbull shook her head, and turned her mouth in to bite her lip. "Maybe when you are better, love–"

"No!" Jim stood up and Ellie saw his mother instinctively flinch. "There's nowt wrong wi' me. I'm not a bloody coward like some people round here. I don' care what you say, nor none of them doctors, there's n…nothin' wrong wi' me!"

Ellie stood up too. "I think I should probably leave." She smiled cautiously at Mrs Turnbull. "Thank you so much for your time, Jim. I really appreciate it."

"I'll show you out, miss," Mrs Turnbull said. Jim sat down again heavily in his seat, his head in his hands, as his mother showed Ellie the few steps to the door.

"I'm sorry if I caused any trouble," Ellie said, as she ducked again under the lintel. "I wouldn't have disturbed you if–"

"It's not your fault, Miss Blaine," she said. "He just–"

Her words were jostled out as Jim pushed past her in the narrow doorway, head down to swing open the low garden gate. Ellie could see the shotgun that had been hanging on the wall was now slung over his shoulder.

"Where do you think you are goin' Jim Turnbull! Come back 'ere at once!" his mother called sharply after him.

He didn't turn around, but carried on striding into the woods that lined that side of the cottage. "I'm going shootin'," he called, his voice disappearing with him into the darkness of the trees. "An' don't wait up for me neither."

Ellie could see Mrs Turnbull's face was etched with concern, and she began to feel her trip to the cottage had achieved nothing more than to upset Jim and worry his mother.

"Is he alright? I didn't upset him, did I?" she asked.

Mrs Turnbull shook her head. "He's not been right, not since Malkie died. Sleeps with his gun by the bed every night, he does. That's if he sleeps at all." She stepped back into the light of the small cottage, half closing the door behind her. "Don't tell no one, I don't want him in no trouble. They'll tek him away, they will."

"I won't," Ellie said. "Perhaps I could ask Richard to see—"

"No!" Mrs Turnbull said sharply. "Please. Don't say a word to his lordship. That would be the worst thing you could do."

Ellie was taken aback by the urgency in Mrs Turnbull's tone. "Why ever would—"

"G'night Miss. You'd best be on your way." The door slammed shut before the words were out and Ellie stood for a moment, until the cottage light went out and the garden fell into darkness. Out in the woods she heard the sharp bark of a shotgun blast, and she turned back towards the hall.

CHAPTER 13

"GOOD mornin' miss, let's get a bit of light in here shall we."

Ellie scrunched up her eyes as Lucy pulled back the shutters and the low morning sun streamed into the room and across the bed where she lay, still in last night's clothes.

"You been out for a walk already?" Lucy said, nodding at the muddy boots dropped by the bedside, matching the dirt that caked the bottom of her trousers and flaked off onto the bed sheets.

"Something like that," Ellie said, sitting up and stretching, squinting at the breakfast of kippers, toast and marmalade that Lucy had brought up. She felt a yearning for pancakes with syrup and a strong mug of coffee.

"Your friend Georgie is here," Lucy continued, pouring out a weak-looking tea into a small bone-china cup. "She and Lord Melmersby are going into town today and I heard her say she'd like your company too, if you forgive me being nosy. Shall I pick out something for you to wear?"

Ellie blinked one tired eye. "Um… yes, of course. Be my guest." She scratched her hair, feeling the tangles and knots and groaning silently at the thought of getting ready in time to join her friend.

"I can help you with that if you like," Lucy said, looking at how Ellie raked her fingers through her hair, stopping to yank a particularly twisted clump.

"Thank you, Lucy, that's very kind, but I don't want to keep you from everything else you have to do."

Lucy swept up a silver-backed brush from the small vanity table in the corner of the room and hopped up onto the bed behind Ellie. "Oh, it's no problem Miss Blaine, I love the chance to do someone's hair."

"You're very good at this," Ellie said, as Lucy gently parted her hair into sections, effortlessly sweeping away tangles Ellie had assumed would be there until she got back to America. "You must have had lots of practice?"

Lucy laughed. "Well, I just like to do it. I never had a little sister, nor even a doll, to practise on so I just make a nuisance of myself when anyone in the house needs brushing."

Ellie returned the laugh. "I can't imagine you doing Lord Melmersby's hair."

"Oh no!" Lucy said, throwing her hands up in mock alarm. "I shouldn't dare to ask him. His brother, mind, when we were little, I'd practice on him all the time. He'd sit ever so patient while I gave him pigtails and little bows. That's 'till he got too big for that and chased me off."

Ellie smiled at the thought of Bertie's blond hair in pigtails. "His hair must have been longer then – or else the pigtails were very short," she said with a chuckle. "And I can't imagine Bertie having the patience to sit there long enough, he never sat still for a minute."

Lucy held out the vanity mirror for Ellie to look at herself, and she caught Lucy's bright smile behind her. "I promise you, he got fed up of me enough times, miss," Lucy said "I made a right nuisance of myself, following him around everywhere. I didn't have no other family, I suppose, 'cept Mrs Madison and she was not much one for play."

Ellie nodded a thank you to Lucy for her work, and she put the mirror down. "I suppose you must miss Bertie?" Ellie said.

"Oh, of course, miss. The place has never been the same since… well, since he was gone."

Ellie stood up to step out of her clothes and into the simple but elegant blue linen dress Lucy had picked out for her local trip. "Thank you Lucy. You have saved the day."

"You look lovely, miss," Lucy said. "I don't think the folk of Melmersby will know what hit them when you walk into Mrs Garnet's Tea Shoppe looking like that."

* * *

"Now that's Mrs Garnet's Tea Shoppe," Georgie said, as she and Ellie walked past the crooked bay window, bordered with neatly-tied blue gingham curtains left open to show a low room full of currently very empty tables and chairs. "We shan't go in there yet as I need to talk to you and it is a veritable den of gossip and scandal."

Ellie laughed. "Do you get much scandal in Melmersby?"

"Not as much as Mrs Garnet would make you believe," Georgie said, taking Ellie's arm to guide her swiftly past the window.

Richard had driven them into Melmersby at Georgie's request so that she could show Ellie around the village while he visited Tom Rabbit, who was still in the lock-up at the local police station while he awaited a court date over the break-in.

"So," Georgie said, checking over her shoulder as they took their walk onto the wide village green and towards the pond where Ellie had scared up the ducks on her first arrival. "The only people who were in or around the house when both Malkie and Vivienne died were you, Richard and Mrs

Madison. Well – I'm counting on it that we can discount you from the equation, which only leaves two people, neither of whom could possibly be a murderer. So perhaps they were both just accidents?"

"Jim was at the house when Malkie died," Ellie said with a shrug. "And his house isn't so far away that he might not have slipped in and out on the night Vivienne died. I saw him last night–"

Georgie's face betrayed something like surprise. "You did?"

"Yes, I called on him and his mother, and she told me – well she told me not to say anything but I trust you to keep it to yourself – she said he was very jumpy since Malkie's death; keeps his gun by his bedside at night."

"How very queer," Georgie said, turning her mouth down curiously. "He does suffer a lot from nerves, since the war, poor chap. Perhaps a death so close to home has simply spooked him?"

"Maybe," Ellie said. "But then I also heard a conversation between Richard and Dr Waterman, where Simon also seemed to be scared – of Richard. It seems they had some falling out years ago, and Richard was trying to reassure him it was all forgotten."

Georgie stopped in her tracks. "Scared of Richard? That doesn't sound like either of them." She started them back on their way again, turning round to walk back to the village street. "They were best of friends years ago, when they trained together. Then something happened. They had a falling out. I have no idea over what. I tried my best to get it out of them, see if I could patch things up between them, but neither of them would say a word about it. What could I do? Richard went away to London, and never returned until his father took sick, just before he died. Oh do watch out for that." Georgie carefully steered Ellie past a fresh-looking obstacle one of the cows who grazed on the village green had recently left in their path.

"They seemed to be getting on at dinner," Ellie said, checking her shoe carefully.

"Well yes. Simon was the one taking care of old Lord Melmersby at the end, and – well, I think Richard appreciated the job he did and it seems they became friends again after that. I can't imagine any old quarrel of theirs would be so bad that Simon would be afraid of Richard. Shall we go in?"

They were back outside the Tea Shoppe and the smell of freshly-baked scones was enough to end the conversation, for now at least. They stepped inside the cluttered room to squeeze into a corner table for two neatly laid with a square tablecloth that matched the curtains.

A tidily dressed and fidgety woman appeared through a beaded curtain at the back of the shop and stepped around the counter, licking her index finger before flipping open a small notebook.

"Good morning, ladies, and what would you like? I know you are partial to a teacake, Miss Parr. Now what would your friend here enjoy? The scones are fresh just now and I have the most delightful blackberry jam that I made with my own hands this last autumn."

"Thank you, Mrs Garnet," Georgie said, "but I've not long breakfasted, so just an Earl Grey with a little lemon for me please. What would you like, Ellie?"

Before she could answer, Mrs Garnet was off again. "Oh, you must be that American girl who is staying up at the Hall. I should have known from the look of you. I am afraid we don't have no American food here, not unless you count biscuits, which you call cookies over there my husband tells me. He's travelled you see, not to America mind, but he heard about it from poor Malkie. He was always so fascinated by America, he was. Said he wanted to go there one day. That was his dream. Malkie, that is, not my husband. My husband's dreams never travel further than the bar of the Royal Oak. Oh look at me, yakking away. What can I get you, love?"

Ellie smiled. "I'll just have the same as Georgie, thank you."

"Of course, what a terrible time for you to visit," Mrs Garnet continued without pausing for breath. "What with poor Mr Fawthrop, and then Vivienne Beauclère. What must you think of the place? It isn't like this usually, I promise you. We don't usually have folk dropping dead like this."

"I'm glad to hear it," Ellie said. "I suppose I was just unlucky with my timing."

Mrs Garnet turned to the kitchen, then suddenly back to the table again. "Of course this is such a quiet village usually. Nothing goes on. And if it does, you can bet I hear about it all in this tea-shop. You'd be surprised how people talk in here. Of course, I'm behind the curtain there, so I can't help but hear what they say. Not that I would listen on purpose, nor ever breathe a word of it to anyone, mind you. I have a saying here: 'what is said in Mrs Garnet's Tea Shoppe stays in Mrs Garnet's Tea Shoppe'. And I keep to that saying as if it were sworn on a holy relic, so I do."

"That's very—"

"I mean, when I heard about poor Malkie, do you know what my first thought was?"

"No, I—"

"I thought: 'well, I'm shocked, but I'm not surprised'. That's what I thought. Of course working on those big dangerous machines with his condition. Well, it's not safe."

"Condition?" Georgie said, narrowing her eyes.

"Well, that's the polite way of saying it. She was the same, of course – Vivienne. They both liked to enjoy themselves, if you know what I mean." Just in case they didn't know what she meant, she demonstrated with a mime of drinking from an invisible glass. "Of course Malkie was barred from the Royal Oak, so perhaps he took to drinking on the job? That would explain it very well."

"Why was he barred?" Ellie asked, glancing at Georgie who shrugged back at her.

"Seems he got into a bit of trouble," Mrs Garnet stopped suddenly. "No, I shouldn't say nothing about something I didn't see with my own eyes. I'm not one for idle gossip."

"Of course not," Georgie said, dryly.

"Well," Mrs Garnet continued, tucking her notebook away in her apron pocket as if accepting she wouldn't be needing it for quite a while yet. "It seems he was bad-mouthing Lord Melmersby – the new one, not the old one. He was very close with the old one you see. Saying something like as how Lord Melm – Dr Richard – had taken something from him. The landlord, who didn't want no trouble with the new lord, he said 'Malkie, you are barred,' and Malkie kicked up a right stink he did. Took two men to take him out. That's how I heard it anyway. Not that I was listening, I just hear things."

"Do you know what it was he thought was taken?" Ellie asked, looking quickly out of the window in case Richard might be returning from his visit with Tom.

"Well, it seems he said that old Lord Melmersby promised him something before he died. Said he had it all official, on paper and everything. But then he was telling everyone how he'd lost whatever it was, and how it was only when Dr Richard returned to the village that he came to lose it. Well, everyone knew what he meant and you can't go accusing the new Lord Melmersby of that kind of thing. I should think the whole story from start to finish was made up after too many pints of

Old Ramsbottom's Ale. Sounds like stuff and nonsense to me."

Ellie looked at Georgie, whose face remained unreadable.

"Oh, look at me, standing here chatting," Mrs Garnet said, picking the notebook back out of her pocket. "You young ladies will be wanting your tea. I shall be back in just a moment."

Mrs Garnet disappeared behind the curtain, while Ellie and Georgie exchanged looks. There were things to be said, but not with only a bead curtain between them and everyone else's business. Instead they washed down their tea with talk of London and the Inns of Court, and Georgie's ambitions. These things she was happy to be spread around the village, if it made one of the little girls now sitting on the pavement outside, vainly waiting their turn with the hoop the boys were keeping to themselves, believe she might have some ambition of her own one day.

After finishing their tea and tipping Mrs Garnet a silver sixpence ("she earned it", Georgia said with a wink) the two women stepped outside, just in time to see the tall figure of Richard striding towards them down the street – shirt sleeves rolled up to his elbows and the bottom half of his trousers dark and dripping with water.

"What on earth have you been up to, Richard?" Georgie said, stepping back to examine the state of his clothes, before leaning in to remove a sliver of duckweed from below his knee.

"Proving young Tom Rabbit's innocence," he said with a satisfied smile, holding out his broad hand to show a rather fine looking blue and gold fountain pen.

"Is that your pen?" Georgie said. "The one that was taken?"

"It is indeed," Richard said, slipping it back into his trouser pocket. "And it was exactly where Tom told me he found the silver cup. Whoever took them – and now I'm sure it wasn't Tom – must have thrown them in the river as they crossed over the bridge."

"Gosh," Georgie said. "So what happens now?"

"Well, right now I am going to fetch the car and take you back to the Hall. Then I shall change my clothes. And then I shall ask Mrs Madison to prepare lunch." Richard smiled and broke into a trot, heading back to the corner by the village church where the car waited. "Oh," he called back, "and Tom Rabbit is a free man, and the police need to start looking elsewhere."

"That seems a peculiar thing to have done if you've gone to all that trouble to steal them?" Georgie said to Ellie as they watched Richard hurry away. "Unless–"

"Unless they only wanted to make it look like they were stealing them," Ellie finished the sentence for her. "Rather than draw attention to whatever they were actually stealing."

"Malkie?"

"My thoughts exactly," Ellie said. "If Richard had taken his paperwork, and he wanted to take it back, where better to look for it than in the study?"

Georgie frowned and shook her head. "Well, that may be, but even if that is true, I am a long way from believing Richard could be a killer. He really is that last man I would imagine... well, he just couldn't be."

Ellie forced a smile. "I'm sure you're right. But something strange is going on, and all of it seems to revolve around him, so if I'm going to find the killer I need to keep digging into what has been going on there."

"If you're going to find the killer?" Georgie said with a sly smile. "You're starting to sound like you might fancy yourself a bit of a detective here. Shall I call you Inspector Blaine?"

The horn on the car sounded as Richard stuttered it down the road towards them, juddering to a halt then lurching forward again.

"I think it rather suits me," Ellie said, smiling. "My first case might be the mystery of why on earth Richard Lindley thought he should be the one to drive us here when he can barely get the car out of first gear!"

CHAPTER 14

"RIGHT, Ellie Blaine, enough of this! We are getting you away from the house and getting you some bracing sea air."

Ellie was busily rearranging the condiments for the fifth time, trying to recreate how the killer (the salt cellar) could sneak up on Malkie (the pepper pot) while he was under the car (the toast rack) without being seen. She looked up at Georgie, momentarily confused.

"At this rate you'll be arresting the kippers. We need a break from all this detection. I've spoken to Richard and he's been an absolute darling and said we can take his car. Mrs Madison is putting together a picnic and I am taking you to Scarborough where we will paddle in the sea, eat too much ice cream and talk nonsense. I'm not taking no for an answer and you have half an hour to get ready."

"But I just—"

"Stop!" Georgie held up a stiff finger to silence Ellie's protestations. "That sounds like you were heading for a 'no' and I just said I'm not taking those today. Get some warm clothes, it's always at least 10 degrees colder in the wind at Scarborough. I shall meet you in the kitchen in precisely 30 minutes."

Ellie stared blankly at her friend, still clutching the pepper pot.

"Chop chop!" Georgie said. "And bring a scarf."

***

Ellie was happy to get back into her driving clothes. The brown leather jacket her father had given her, that had kept the wind off on deck on the sea voyage over, was something of a comfort blanket. Which explained why it was frayed at the sleeves, and a little cracked and worn in general. But it kept out the cold and it made her feel more like herself again, so it was the perfect choice for a break from Melmersby.

She checked herself in the bedroom mirror, turning up the jacket collar with a grin, then took the corridor again to the stairs and down through the house to the kitchens. Passing the wide window of the entrance hall, she caught sight of Richard pacing the lawn and looking up at the higher windows above, his hand shielding his eyes from the mid-morning sun. Walking into the kitchen, she could see Georgie talking with Mrs Madison, whose attention was focused on a growing pile of sandwiches on the table.

"Ah, Ellie. Splendid!" Georgie said, tossing the car keys in her hand. "Right on time. Mrs Madison has made the most delightful spread for us. Shall we get packed and on our way?"

"Oh, it's nothing," Mrs Madison said, batting away the compliment. "I just put a few bits and pieces together and– Mr Madison! Get off that at once!"

Mrs Madison waved a tea towel frantically at the cat, who had rushed in through the open kitchen door to jump up onto the table and was sniffing at the corner of a large door-step sandwich. He jumped back a little as the towel flicked past his ear, then suddenly lunged forward, pulling out a thick piece of chicken from between two slices of bread, and disappearing under the table.

'Mr Madison! You are a very naughty boy!" Mrs Madison shouted, her voice unnaturally high. "I should give you a good hiding for that you beastly–"

Mr Madison appeared from under the table, the chicken safely in his fat, ginger belly; purring loudly and rubbing against the housekeeper's thick ankles.

"I'm so sorry, Miss Parr," She said. "He must have heard your keys, he thinks it's dinner time when he hears that sound and he's so fast, I didn't have time to stop him." She scowled at the cat as he licked his lips. "Mr Madison! You will be the death of me. That was for the picnic. Oh, I can't stay mad at you." Mrs Madison picked him up and buried her face in his thick fur to give him a hearty kiss. If Ellie didn't know better, she could have sworn the cat winked at her.

"I'll help you get these packed up," Ellie said, starting to fold a clean muslin cloth over the remaining sandwiches.

"Don't you trouble yourself now," Mrs Madison said. "There's a way to do this properly and I shall imagine you'd just make a mess of it."

Ellie shot a glance at Georgie as if to say "is she always this rude?", and received one back that could only mean "yes, she is".

"Um, thanks. I think." Ellie said. "We should probably best get going then, Georgie."

Georgie nodded, as Mrs Madison neatly folded the sandwiches into a perfect square that slotted exactly into the remaining space of a well-packed wicker basket.

"There you go," she said, standing back to admire her handiwork. "Now you go and enjoy yourselves and have a lovely day at the seaside."

"Thank you, Mrs Madison," Ellie said, a genuine smile breaking out at the housekeepers sudden friendliness, "I'm sure we—"

"Course, I'd love to go to the seaside but I never get the chance myself," she cut in. "Too busy working the kitchens, running the house, cleaning up after everyone. Never get a break myself, can't remember the last time I had so much as a weekend away."

"I see," Ellie said, taking a step back towards the kitchen door. "Maybe if—"

"Of course Lucy — that's a different story. But then she always was Richard's favourite. Well, I'm just an old woman aren't I, I'm no one's favourite. Least 'cept for Mr Madison. He cares about me."

"I'm sure—"

"I mean, I understand Lucy was upset, what with Malkie and all, but how come as she gets the week off and away she goes to Harrogate, no expense spared? I was shocked too, but oh, no one thinks of old Mrs Madison do they? She just soldiers on, no need for her to have a break."

Ellie thought it best not to try to interrupt again, and fixed as sympathetic a look on her face as she could while Mrs Madison carried on, waving the tea towel about her as she spoke.

"I wouldn't mind, only he already gave Lucy time off to go to York last month, when she said she was feeling tired. Tired? I can tell you about tired. I would like a long weekend in York too, if you don't mind, not that anyone asked me. And that place she stayed at don't come cheap, I can tell you that too; she won't have paid for that neither, not on her wages. Crown Hotel — do you know how much that place costs? I ask you! He spoils her, he does. And nothing good comes of spoiling no-one 'cept to make 'em lazy and forget about those what does the hard graft of looking after them the rest of the time."

Ellie was beginning to wonder if their day out might be over before Mrs Madison stopped talking, when Georgie suddenly stepped in.

"You don't get the appreciation you deserve, Mrs Madison. I shall go right this minute and tell Richard exactly what a beast he has been to you, and how upset you are about it."

Mrs Madison's pink cheeks suddenly shook off a little of their colour. "Oh no, oh my. Don't you go bothering his lordship, it's just silly old Mrs Madison talking her mouth off again. No, don't you worry dear. I don't even like York, nor Harrogate. Full of snobs they are. You just go off and have a nice time at the seaside. Don't mind me." She picked up a spotlessly clean casserole dish that had been sitting on the table and began urgently polishing it with her tea towel.

"Thank you, we will," Georgie said. "And thank you once again for your splendid spread." Georgie quickly glanced at Ellie and nodded towards the kitchen door.

Ellie slipped through the door, while Georgie gathered up the picnic supplies, and quickly made her way back through the house the way that she knew led out into the grounds and the garage. Just as she was passing through into the gardens, she almost bumped head-first into Lucy, who was coming the other way with a small basket of fresh herbs.

"Oh sorry, miss. Didn't see you there."

Ellie nodded an apology. "My fault, I wasn't looking."

Lucy smiled, then looked at Ellie's tattered driving jacket. "You going out for a spin, miss? Anywhere nice?"

"Scarborough, I think. Do you know it?"

Lucy hesitated for a second. "It's a lovely place, miss. I went there with Bertie a few times. When we were younger, you know. It's really a lovely place. Be sure to take a walk up to the Spa, the tea rooms there are really nice."

Ellie couldn't help but notice Lucy's face redden as she spoke, and thought her own expression might have reflected this as Lucy quickly offered an explanation that hadn't been asked for.

"He was very kind to take me out in his car sometimes, just for a drive, that's all. I don't want you thinking– I should probably just get these herbs to the kitchen, Mrs Madison was wanting them bringing quickly you know. I should…"

Ellie smiled kindly. "I'll make sure I visit the Spa, thank you."

Lucy nimbly stepped around her into the house, closing the door behind her. For a second Ellie stared at the closed door, then shook her head and carried on her walk to the garage.

***

Richard's own car was a small but elegant tourer — built by Charron-Laycock, he had told Ellie. It was considerably more comfortable, but somewhat slower, than the Sunbeam that had made an end of poor Malkie, and Georgie — at least — was grateful for that, with Ellie at the wheel all the way to Scarborough.

"Remember, it's not a race," Georgie said, as they pulled out of the driveway and onto the narrow road into the village.

Ellie laughed. "Don't worry, I'll take it steady. We're not in a hurry are we?"

The road leading back into the village was shining from a fresh spring shower that had made a very brief pass over Melmersby Hall while Ellie got the car out of the garage. The trees that lined the road on the estate side dripped water that splashed a rat-a-tat on the car's canvas roof, while on the left of the road, the little river that would turn under the bridge ahead was overspilling its banks as it ran through the middle of broad cow pastures.

"Careful at the bend now," Georgie said nervously as the car passed through the village, splashing up water onto the stone flags of the empty High Street.

"Oh, I know all about that now," Ellie said, as the car rose up over the hump of the bridge, sending Georgie's stomach into a flutter.

She gently squeezed the brakes, bringing the car to almost walking pace, as the road turned into the hairpin bend that wrapped around the little oxbow duck pond. The road was only a little wider than the car here, and Ellie kept it close to the left side as she turned, in case anything was coming the other way.

Suddenly, as the bend opened up, she spotted the figure of a man standing next to the verge, almost directly in their path. Luckily, she'd taken the turn cautiously enough that she had time to stamp on the brakes and bring the car to a sudden stop with only a slight jolt of her passenger.

"What on earth? Jim – what are you doing, you'll get yourself killed. Didn't you hear us coming?"

Georgie was busily rearranging her hat and driving glasses, while Ellie shook her head at Jim Turnbull, now leaning, unbalanced, back into the wet hawthorn hedge that lined the roadside.

"I'm s…sorry, miss. I was just l…lookin' for r…rabbits. I weren't payin' no attention to the r…road. Begin' your pardon, miss."

Jim hauled himself up from the hedge, pulling up the strap of his shotgun that had tangled itself in the briars.

"Just be careful," Ellie said gently. "If I'd been going any faster it might have been a nasty accident."

Jim nodded apologetically and raised his hand to them as Ellie pulled slowly away.

"I've no idea why he's in the road," Georgie said, still straightening her scarf. "There's a footpath that cuts along the river all the way back to the estate – that's twice as quick and ten times as safe. He must have a death wish."

Ellie shrugged. "Looking for rabbits, I guess? Like he said. I'm starting to dislike that bend."

The road opened up ahead of them, and the shower clouds parted to reveal a sunny spring day. The warm, wet ground sent up an earthy smell that mingled with the scent of oil and leather in the car. Ellie shifted gear as they approached a short, steep hill and Georgie put her hand on top of hers, as if to reassure her that they were leaving any troubles behind in Melmersby, at least for today.

As the landscape of north Yorkshire rolled by, Ellie's thoughts went back for a moment to her meeting with Lucy as she left the house.

"Georgie?" she said. "Can I ask you something?"

"Of course. What is it?"

She hesitated a moment. "I just wondered. Lucy said something back there. I suppose, what I mean is… were she and Bertie ever… you know?"

Georgie gave a short, sharp laugh. "Lovers?" she said, emphasising the word as if reading from a scandal sheet.

Ellie turned to look at Georgie, trying to read her face. "Well, yes." She felt awkward asking. She knew there had been others before her, she was never concerned about that, but it suddenly seemed close to home. "Not that it matters, I suppose."

"Well!" Georgie said brightly, sitting up straight in her seat as if about to deliver a thrilling tale. "I wouldn't go that far, but there was quite the little scandal when they were younger. All perfectly innocent though."

"Go on?" Ellie said cautiously, half frowning and half smiling.

"Well, I'm sure you know, Lucy and Bertie were great friends growing up together. Of course, when he got a bit older Bertie suddenly found he was far too grown-up to play with girls any more. Poor Lucy was heartbroken, of course. She absolutely doted on him and followed him everywhere, but he would shoo her away when the other boys came over. Of course, then she got a bit older and, well…"

"She is very pretty," Ellie said wryly.

"Indeed. So suddenly Bertie didn't seem so keen to shoo her away anymore. I suppose he must have been 18, she was 16, at the time. He'd just got his first car and he took her out driving a few times. All very sweet and innocent, back before supper time and all that. But you could see there was a little spark there – certainly all the girls who'd set their sights on Bertie saw it."

"So what happened?" Ellie asked.

"Well, apparently, after one particular trip to Scarborough, Lucy couldn't help but tell Mrs Madison that she and Bertie had kissed. Well, needless to say, Mrs Madison wasn't having that and so she told Lord Melmersby and he was absolutely furious. You'd think his son had eloped with a tinker's daughter to hear him. He called a meeting with Bertie – all very official – and invited Dr Waterman along too."

"Simon?" Ellie said, surprised.

"Oh no, Simon is little older than Bertie. His father, the Lindley family doctor – a great, grumpy bear of a physician who liked to dress, and act, as if old Queen Victoria was still in the prime of her youth. Terrifying man! I'm sure they both lectured him on 'the unsuitability of breeding with the lower classes' or some other dreadful nonsense. Anyway, whatever it was, it seemed to do the trick and that was the end of that for Bertie and Lucy."

Ellie shook her head thoughtfully. "Poor Lucy, she must have been upset?"

"She was, at first," Georgie said. "But she seemed to get over it pretty quickly. They stayed great friends to the end. She was about the only girl in the village who seemed genuinely happy for him when he became engaged to you. Like I say, I don't think it was much more than a rather sweet little crush."

Ellie smiled. She remembered what Bertie had told her about Lucy when they were together. Not much, but she could tell he had real affection for her, and she felt suddenly grateful to her for being there for him growing up. She felt a little something fade away in her chest, and pulled herself up when she realised it must have been jealousy. Just a little, she was sure, but it had been there.

* * *

Georgie had been right, Ellie thought as she pulled her jacket collar up tighter to her throat, it was a lot colder in Scarborough. The wind whipped up from the sea to sting her ears, even with the sun still shining in the clear sky above. They'd decided against the Spa: "far too full of tourists and dreadful brass bands playing out of tune," Georgie had told her. Instead, they'd found a spot on the beach to roll out their picnic mat and hired a wind-breaker which did little to hold off the cold. Georgie had gone to collect another, for double protection against the elements, while Ellie's thoughts ran from the weather and the delicious sandwiches and back towards events at Melmersby.

"Ellie! I hope you aren't doing what I think you are with that spoon." Georgie had appeared suddenly behind her and was scowling at the cutlery in her hands.

"Um..."

"Who exactly is that fork meant to be?" Georgie said, folding her arms stiffly.

"Richard," Ellie sighed apologetically.

"The whole point of this trip was to stop you playing detective and give your over-active brain a rest, darling." Georgie sat down heavily in the sand next to her and held her hand out for Ellie to pass her the 'suspects'.

"It's just. I've been thinking..."

"Don't!" Georgie snapped. "At least not today. Let's get an ice cream or something; cool that fevered curiosity of yours."

Ellie picked up a half a carrot. "Suppose this is Vivienne…"

"Oh lord!" Georgie sighed. "Alright, let's go along with this and get it over with. So what is Carrot Vivienne doing?"

Ellie shrugged. "Well, she's dead."

Georgie closed her eyes and shook her head.

"But Fork Rich – Richard, you see, he and Archie: it must have been one of them."

"One of them?"

"Yes – who put the feather in her hand."

Georgie lifted her head back, raising her eyebrows as high as they would go. "And why do you say that?"

"Well," Ellie said, taking back the spoon from Georgie's open hand. "If we assume the killer is leaving feathers on his victims, why would Vivienne take the feather from someone deliberately and hold onto it all the while she was dying? So, we can assume that the feather was put in her hand after she died."

Georgie's expression suddenly changed from incredulity to something more like interest. "Go on?"

"We know the only two people who went near her after she left the dinner party were Richard, when he was checking on her pulse, and then her husband. So it stands to reason one of them must have put the feather in her hand."

Georgie shook her head. "But it doesn't make sense? Why would either of them want to kill her?"

"You said yourself, Archie was a philanderer, a cad. The way Vivienne was talking at the dinner table, perhaps she planned to divorce him finally? She'd had enough. He stood to lose all the money that he got from her. So he bumped her off before she could cut him off!" Ellie threw down the spoon theatrically.

"Sorry, Inspector Blaine, but that doesn't hold up," Georgie said, putting the spoon carefully back into an inside pocket of the picnic basket.

"Why ever not?" Ellie said. "Seems as good a motive as any, I don't see who else would gain from her death."

"Pretty much everyone would get something," Georgie said dryly. "Everyone except Archie."

"Except Archie?" Ellie reached for the spoon again and Georgie gently slapped her hand.

"Vivienne's money all came from her family. Yes, she was loaded, but she didn't earn a penny herself – it was all daddy's money. And daddy, I can promise you, absolutely loathes Archie. Right now he is in the process of having his son-in-law turfed out of Vivienne's home without so much as a brass farthing to his name. And Archie would have known that was exactly how it would be. You saw how upset he was about his wife's death – that wasn't because he loved her; Lord knows he doesn't have the capacity to love anyone but himself. That was because he saw his little gravy train going off the rails. I can promise you, Archie would be the last person on earth to kill Vivienne."

Ellie held up the fork nervously. "So that just leaves…"

"Richard?" Georgie said, shaking her head rapidly. "Absolutely not. No, not a chance."

"Why are you so sure?"

Georgie took the fork from Ellie's hand and put it back alongside the suspect spoon. "Because he is not someone who would ever take a life. He pretty much gave up everything for that very reason."

Ellie sat back into the soft sand. "What do you mean?"

Georgie sat lower too, resting her weight behind her on her hands. "Richard was disowned by his father, cut off, for it, and it was the reason he left Yorkshire. All because he wouldn't take a life, under any circumstances. When the war came, when the call went out for men; Bertie signed up straight away but Richard didn't. He wouldn't. His conscience wouldn't let him. He refused to fight."

Ellie blanched. "But I thought…"

"So his father called him a coward. When Bertie died, then his mother – from a broken heart, his father believed – old Lord Melmersby blamed him for both and told Richard he was no longer his son and he should never return to the family home."

Ellie's mind began to race. Richard had told her he was there in the trenches when Bertie died. Had that all been a lie then? A means to gain her trust? For what? And, if he was disowned by his father, why then was he now Lord Melmersby, and inherited the whole estate? Unless there was no will. Or unless a will had gone missing.

"We should get back," Ellie said. "It's getting late."

Georgie looked up at the sun, lower now in the sky, picking out the coastline behind them. "I suppose we should," she said. "But look, no more talk of suspects please. And certainly get it out of your head that Richard might have had anything to do with this. I know he can seem a little cold at times, but he is a very good man and take it from someone who knows him as well as anyone: he is not a killer, and I won't hear any more about it."

Georgie stood up and put out her hand to help Ellie to her feet. She nodded thanks then silently helped with packing the rest of the picnic away.

The sun was almost down by the time they walked back up the hill to the car. Ellie was still lost in thought as she turned the key and lit up the headlights.

"Everything alright?" Georgie asked, leaning in a little to catch Ellie's expression in the half-light.

"Yes, absolutely," she said firmly. "It's just been a long day. Let's get going. I've got a few things to catch up on when we get back to Melmersby Hall."

ELLIE BLAINE 1920s MYSTERIES

CHAPTER 15

THE conversation was sparse on the drive back home. The sea air had made her tired and she needed to concentrate on the road, Ellie had said. But in reality her mind was wide awake to the possibility that the man whose house she was now staying in − the man who might have been her brother-in-law − was a killer. And if no one would believe her, then she needed to find something that would prove her right.

It was late when they arrived back at Melmersby Hall. Georgie needed to leave early for London in the morning and so she went straight to bed, while Ellie stayed up a little longer by the light of a coloured-glass lamp, nursing a stale scotch and a growing sense of suspicion.

The clock above the fireplace in the lounge showed it was well past midnight as Ellie drained the last of her whisky and quietly put the glass down. The house was quiet, but for the occasional creak as the old floorboards above her contracted with the falling temperature of the night air. Somewhere up there, she thought, the household were all asleep – and one of them, quite possibly, might be troubled with dreams of just what they did to Malkie and Vivienne.

Something else might be up there too. The proof she needed to confirm her suspicions. If Malkie did break into the study, he was looking for something important. Something important enough that he was killed for it. If she was going to find out what that was, there was really only one place she could start, and if Malkie didn't find it, maybe she would have more luck. She knew where the study was, she had seen Richard coming out of it on her first day at the Hall. Unfortunately, she also knew it was on the same corridor, and very close to, the room where Richard would now be sleeping. She would need to be quiet, and she would need to be cautious.

* * *

The creaking of the old house would give her some cover at least; everyone was so used to the noises it made in the night that they would sleep through any she might make as she tiptoed along the corridor that led to the study. That was the good news; the bad was that there were no windows on this corridor to let in even a little moonlight, and so she was in complete and utter darkness, needing to feel her way along the wall for the door she needed. Not the first one – that would be the guest room where Vivienne and Archie had slept the night before her death. The study was the next one along just past this–

Ellie froze; her foot half-down on a loose board that let out an almighty groan as it creaked out of place. She tried to pull her foot back slowly, but it squeaked just as hard in that direction. To her left, she heard the sound of movement in a bed, then a man's deep cough.

For a moment she was caught in two minds, both equally unsure. She could bluff it – stride along the corridor even more loudly, then explain to Richard she had simply lost her way, in the dark, without turning on the lights. No, that wouldn't work.

Or she could sit still until he went back to sleep. But if he didn't; if instead he opened the door and saw her crouched down in the darkened corridor right outside his room? Well, that really would take some explaining.

The coughing stopped, and she heard the sound of someone turning in their bed, then silence. She held her breath for what seemed like minutes, then lifted the last of the pressure of her foot from the tell-tale board. To her relief, it seemed it had already given out most of its creaking and – after a couple more minutes of waiting, just for luck – she moved the last few yards down the corridor until her left hand felt the hard wood of what must be the study door. She turned the handle and gave a light tug - unsurprised to find it locked, but ready for that eventuality.

She took a hairpin from her bag. She'd learned a few tricks growing up with the racers and gamblers of the track, and this was a favourite – gently feeling for the tumblers in the lock, she eased them in the right direction with a satisfying click.

She was relieved to find the hinges were a little less rusty than some others in the house as she quietly turned the handle and pushed the door ajar, slipping into the room before gently closing it behind her. Her hand felt along the wall for the shape of a light switch, which she flipped on with a nervous click.

The light made her scrunch up her eyes for a second while they adjusted after so long in the dark. When she opened them fully, she could see the study was a small room – lined all around with bookcases and shelves that made the space feel even smaller. There was a single sash window directly opposite the door, with the frame slightly cracked by the marks of a forced entry. The shelves were filled with boxes and stacks of paper; some bound, others just loosely placed one on top to the other. From the covering of dust, there seemed little sign that any of these had been disturbed in a long while. If someone had broken into this room to find something, they must surely have known exactly what they were looking for and exactly where to find it.

She looked around carefully for any sign that something had been touched, when her eyes caught fresh wood splinters around the lock of one of the cabinets. "That must be it," she thought – the only sign other than the broken window frame that someone had been here. She pulled at the door of the cabinet and it swung open to reveal: more folders full of papers. Again, none of them seemed to have been disturbed, though it was harder to tell as the closed cabinet had kept the dust off these. She carefully read the labels on the folders; all written with an old-fashioned hand in dark, India ink: *"Accounts of the Melmersby Estate: 1897-8"; "Matters pertaining to the personal health of Master Bertram Bartholomew Alexander Lindley"; "Employment Records 1912-13"; "Household and livery expenses 1914"* – folder after folder of dry, dusty family and estate records, all ordered by year. She wasn't sure what she'd expected to find, she just felt a little disappointed in what she had.

It was possible, she thought, that Lord Melmersby might have left a record of any will among these; but if he had, either the thief had found it quickly or been disturbed themselves before they could rummage through them as they were all still neatly filed together. Either way, it seemed unlikely.

She glanced around the room again, hoping to find some more obvious sign of the thief's quarry, when her eye caught a small, rectangular, leather case on the top of one of the high shelves. It looked out of place; not least because it was the only thing in the room not covered in dust. Ellie pulled out the dark-wood chair that had been pushed under a cluttered writing desk, positioning it below the shelf where she could step on it to reach up higher. One leg of the chair was evidently a little shorter than the others, or else the floor was crooked, either way her improvised ladder wobbled unnervingly below her as she stretched out her fingers to try to catch the handle of the case. Just too high – not for the first time, she wished she might not have inherited her father's lack of height along with his driving skills. While she couldn't reach the box, she was now close enough to read the label: '*Richard JA Lindley: Dr. RAMC*'.

"I just need another inch," she said to herself, looking around urgently for something she could use to add the extra height. On the floor, next to where she had put her chair, she saw a sturdy looking book bound in blue leather. "That'll do," she said, hopping down to reach it. No sooner had her feet hit the ground than she heard the unmistakable sound of a door handle turning across the corridor, and the creak of hinges.

"Hello? Is anyone there?" Richard's voice.

"Damn!" she hissed to herself. She looked around frantically for a hiding place, but any available space was already clogged up with books and papers. There was only one option – the same one the thief must have taken. Ellie frantically worked her fingers under the crack in the window frame and heaved. She heard footsteps in the corridor and just had time to flick off the light switch and get back across the room to slide through the gap in the window, before she heard the study door open. The room was on the first floor, but she was relieved to find that the old ivy that covered the whole of this side of the house was sturdy enough to take her weight as she clung to it just below and under the mantle of the window.

"Hmm," she heard the confused grunt from above her. "I thought I'd closed that."

The mantle hid her from the view of the window, or at least it would so long as Richard didn't lean his head out. She heard the sound of the window opening wider and she held her breath. After a moment, made all the more awkward by the particularly hairy wolf spider that had now crawled out of its ivy nest and was making its way along her arm, she heard the sash window slam shut. She let out a sharp puff – partly in relief and partly to blow away the creature that was now almost up to her shoulder.

She scrambled down the short drop to the driveway below, losing her footing at the last moment to crumple and crunch, bottom-down, into the deep shingle. One of the bushes that lined the house shuddered behind her, and the familiar figure of a fat ginger cat appeared; staring at her briefly before trotting up, tail held high, to nuzzle her arm with his cold nose.

"Hello Mr Madison," she said. "That was not my most dignified exit!"

"Miss Blaine? What on earth— are you alright miss?" Ellie's head turned sharply at the voice, to see Lucy, wrapped in a simple but elegant dressing gown and holding an old-fashioned oil lamp.

"Sorry, Lucy,' Ellie said, sheepishly pulling herself up from the ground. "I couldn't sleep, I was just taking a walk and I... tripped. Over Mr Madison." She looked guiltily down at the cat who seemed happy enough to go along with the story and continued to rub his broad cheeks against her legs.

"Well, you be careful, miss," she said. "Don't you go hurting yourself. I heard a noise out here and I thought we had another burglar on our hands, I was just about to call the police. You gave me quite a start!"

Ellie bowed her head in a sign of apology as Lucy turned back to the house and called Mr Madison to get back to his bed too. The cat was unmoved, sniffing at Ellie's slippered feet curiously and ignoring the calls as Lucy slipped back through the door into her quarters.

Mr Madison suddenly put back his ears and put up his tail, looking up warily at a large rhododendron bush that sat on the edge of the wide lawn. His back arched and he let out a sharp hiss.

"What is it, puss?" Ellie said, squinting into the darkness. She took a step towards the bush and, as she did, the leaves suddenly moved. In the movement, the moonlight caught something: a glint, barely there for a second, but long enough for her to make out the glow of a lit cigarette end. The light disappeared just as quickly, to the sound of cracking branches and heavy feet, as a figure sprinted away back into the cover of trees and the darkness.

Mr Madison let out a sharp "meow" in the direction of the running figure and Ellie bent down to scratch at his ear reassuringly.

"I agree with you, Mr Madison," she said. "We should get inside. It's starting to feel a little dangerous around here."

ELLIE BLAINE 1920s MYSTERIES

CHAPTER 16

WHAT little sleep Ellie was able to snatch was fitful. Her mind raced along a dozen different roads: did Richard know she was in the study last night?; if so, was she now in danger?; who was it hiding in the bushes, and what were they doing there?; what was in the leather case in the study, and how could she get back in to find out?; might it just be easier to let the police deal with this and get back to Indiana as quickly as possible?

"No!" she called out loud to herself, sitting up suddenly in bed. She looked around to check no one was there to hear her shouting at herself. "If I just find out what's in the case," she thought, keeping the words to herself this time. "I'm sure that will be important. I'll wait until Richard is out, look in the case, and tell the police whatever I find. Then that's it – I'm done."

The thought shook her out of her half-sleep and she jumped up in bed to swing her legs over the side. There was already a pot of tea and some cold, buttered toast by the side of her bed. Lucy must have brought them in without waking her, she thought. The tea was as cold as the toast, but she drank down a cup anyway to ease her dry throat.

She washed her face, grimacing a little at just how tired she looked in the mirror with the morning light on her face, then put on a simple house dress and flat shoes to walk downstairs. She felt a little nervous at the thought of bumping into Richard, and straightened her back to practice a show of confident nonchalance that might hide any guilt showing in her face. But he had left early and wasn't home, it seemed. Instead, she walked into the lounge to see Mrs Madison and Lucy sat alongside each other on the green leather sofa, facing a serious-looking Detective Inspector Lochner, who stood politely to greet her.

"Good morning, Miss Blaine. I hope you are well," he said, his hand briefly reaching to lift a hat, before he remembered it was currently sitting on the chess table rather than his head. "I was just asking these ladies some questions regarding the unfortunate events of the last few days. Perhaps you would care to join us?"

"Of course," Ellie said, setting herself down in a small, slightly uncomfortable, sewing chair that was squeezed between the sofa and the window. She smiled at the two women, Mrs Madison stern-faced and silent, Lucy offering a weak smile back, in between biting at her short nails.

"Now Lucy, could you continue where you left off?" DI Lochner said, flipping over a page in his small notebook and lifting his pencil to hover over it. "You said this happened when?"

"It would have been about 5 years ago, sir. Yes, that's right – it was just a few weeks after Bertie had gone back to France after his leave for Christmas, so early 1916 I would say," Lucy said, biting harder now.

DI Lochner nodded, brow furrowed as he scrawled in the notebook. "And you say you saw an incident, involving the three victims and Dr Lindley?"

"Three?" Ellie said suddenly.

"Yes," DI Lochner said solemnly, "well, two for certain, one we are still investigating."

Ellie shook her head. "Who is the third?"

"Dr Waterman," Mrs Madison said, her brow creased. "His wife called here earlier to see if he was here. She is beside herself with worry."

"Simon is dead?" Ellie said, looking from Mrs Madison to the inspector. Lucy buried her head in her hands.

"Well, we don't know that for sure," DI Lochner said with a stern look at Mrs Madison who now had her arms folded and her ample chest puffed out. "He's missing. His car was found abandoned out by the old quarry lake after he didn't come home last night. And there are further suspicious circumstances."

"Suspicious?" Ellie said.

Mrs Madison went to speak again, but the inspector silenced her with a raised finger so that he could speak. "Yes. It appears Dr Waterman received a letter shortly before his disappearance which leads us to believe there may be a connection with the deaths of Malkie Fawthrop and Vivienne Beauclère."

"What did the letter say?" Ellie asked, leaning forward.

"I'm afraid that as this is an active inquiry I am not at liberty to—"

"There was a feather in it. That's all. Just a feather, that's what Mrs Waterman told me," Mrs Madison blurted out. "Same as those other two. There's something awful going on here I tell you, none of us is safe no more!"

DI Lochner shook his head slowly and sighed. "Well, it seems that particular piece of information is no longer under wraps, so yes, it was a feather. A white feather, just like the others. Which is where I was in my discussion with young Lucy here, if you could please continue." He gestured towards Lucy with his open hand and she sat up straight.

"Well yes, sir. Like I said it was early 1916, maybe January or February. I remember there was snow on the ground. Anyway, Dr Richard was up from London while Bertie was home and he had stayed on a while, at his mother's asking I think. The night before he left, I had heard a terrible row between Dr Richard and his father, and Dr Waterman was there too. I didn't listen to none of it, honest, but it was about the war I think. The next day Dr Richard was all set to leave, with his bags packed and so on, waiting for the car to take him to the station. I— I don't feel right saying this."

"Please carry on, Lucy, this is important," DI Lochner said. Ellie reached across and squeezed Lucy's hand and she nodded.

"Well, I shouldn't really have been there but I had forgotten the mop-head for cleaning the landing in the west wing and it was back in the kitchen. So I was at the top of the stairs when I saw them. Malkie came in first, and I was thinking he was just come in to pick up the bags to take to the car, but right behind him was Dr Waterman and Miss Summerville — that was Vivienne before she married Archie, when she was still engaged to Dr Lindley. Anyhow, all three of them were there and they were talking ever so serious to Dr Lindley and then—" Lucy's voice caught up in a sob and her hand rose to wipe the teardrops that were now breaking loose from her eyes.

Mrs Madison looked at her, unmoving, while Ellie sat on the arm of the sofa and put her arm around her shoulder. "It's ok, Lucy," she said. "I'm sure the inspector can hear the rest of it later."

"I'm alright, thank you," Lucy said, sniffing hard and shaking out her shoulders. "It's just. I didn't think anything of it until… until Dr Waterman. You see it was the same three. They all gave him something, each of them, one after the other."

"And what did they give him?" DI Lochner said. "Did you see?"

Lucy sighed deeply, her breath shuddering. "I did, sir. It was feathers, sir. All three of them gave him a white feather."

Ellie took her arm from Lucy's shoulder and sat back into her small chair, silent for a moment.

"And did you tell anyone of this? Have you ever told anyone, apart from those of us here today, what you saw?" DI Lochner said, his tone even more serious now.

Lucy shook her head. "Not a soul, sir. I didn't think it was my place to say nothing. I swear, sir, I never told nobody."

DI Lochner closed his notebook deliberately, dropping his pencil back into his top jacket pocket. "Thank you very much Lucy, that will be all for now. Dr Lindley is currently in Sidthorpe, covering Dr Waterman's surgery while he is…unavailable. I shall be talking to him later this evening, but I would ask all of you here to promise me not to breathe a word of this to anyone. I cannot stress how important this is, lives may be at stake. Possibly even your own."

Mrs Madison let out a gargled cry and Lucy, already softly sobbing, sank back into the sofa until it almost seemed she was buried in it.

"Why feathers?" Ellie said to the inspector who was already starting to stand up.

DI Lochner straightened out the folds in his trousers and tucked his shirt back in where the tails had ridden out. "For cowardice, miss."

"Cowardice?"

"Yes miss," the inspector picked up his hat. "Now, I'm not saying Dr Lindley is a coward. I would never say that and I know him not to be. But at the time, what with the war and so many good men dead, there was a lot of emotion about in the country. I believe those feathers were meant as a sign of cowardice, on account of Dr Lindley being a conchy and all."

"A conchy?" Ellie said, shaking her head.

"Conscientious Objector, miss. Those who wouldn't fight, for reasons of their conscience. Dr Lindley, I believe, refused on the grounds of having taken his oath as a doctor not to harm no-one. But, as we've heard here, some people would not accept that. Sadly, some still don't, but that's as may be. I'm not one to judge."

Ellie left the two women on the sofa while she showed the inspector to the door. She glanced back in their direction cautiously, and spoke quietly. "Do you think Richard killed them," she said, turning the handle to crack the door open. "Malkie, Vivienne, Simon – in revenge?"

Inspector Lochner put his hat firmly back on his head and took the door, opening it wide enough to step through. "There are a number of lines of inquiry ongoing at the moment, miss, and we take each on its merits. I would ask you to take care to not say any of this to Dr Lindley on his return, and while we don't believe you to be in any particular danger, I would ask you to be cautious of your own person while at Melmersby Hall and not to put yourself into a situation where you might find yourself at risk. You can call me or PC Wade at the station at any time you might need us, or if you have any further information you believe might help our inquiries. Good day, Miss Blaine."

DI Lochner handed a card with a telephone number scrawled on it to Ellie, then raised his hat deliberately before stepping through the door. She closed the door behind him, then leant back against it, gathering her thoughts. Perhaps this wasn't about any inheritance after all, just cold vengeance? But then what was the thief looking for in the study, and what was in that case, and how did any of that fit a simple, but brutal, revenge plot? No matter what DI Lochner said, she would have to put herself into a situation of risk if she was to find out. And she'd need to do it soon, before Richard got back.

She walked back into the lounge to find Mrs Madison had left Lucy alone on the sofa. She was quietly talking to herself, shaking her head and picking at her nails that she had bitten down to the quick.

"Are you feeling alright, Lucy?" Ellie said softly.

Lucy sat up with a start. "Oh, Lord! Miss! You gave me a scare, I didn't see you there."

"Sorry," Ellie said, "You did the right thing, you know, saying what you saw. Even if it doesn't feel like it now."

Lucy stood up, shaking her head swiftly from side to side, as if shaking out a thought. "Anyway, I can't go around feeling sorry for myself can I? I got work to do. And I promised Jim I'd pop in and see him with his little comfort parcel, he relies on me and I can't let him down. I must get going, oh where did I put everything?"

Ellie stepped aside to let her past. "I don't suppose you know what time Richard will be back, do you?" she called after her.

"Dr Waterman's surgery finishes at 4," Lucy said, stopping suddenly to look around before picking up an apple from the fruit bowl on the walnut-topped table beside the lounge door. "So he should be back here by 4:45 at the latest I would say."

"Thank you," Ellie said. Four forty five? That gave her a good six hours at least to do a little more digging in the study. But she'd need to wait for Mrs Madison to finish her cleaning and be back in the kitchens, just in case. If Richard was the killer, if it was revenge, then the three people who gave him the feathers were already taken care of. The only person he'd have any need of killing now would be someone who found evidence to see him convicted for his crimes.

"Why do you do this to yourself, Ellie?" she said under her breath. She thought of her father, and the thrill, the uncertainty, of the race track – that thin, dazzling knife-edge on which you balance between triumph and disaster, the difference between living and feeling alive. She sighed. "I miss you, Dad," she said, looking up. "But sometimes I wish you'd been a plumber."

CHAPTER 17

THE smell of suet crust and boiled beef was wafting through the house, which could mean only one thing. Mrs Madison would be tied up for the next couple of hours and this was her chance. Lucy was still not back from her trip out to Jim's cottage, Richard wouldn't be back for another three hours. It was now or never. Double-checking that the kitchen door was firmly closed, Ellie quietly made her way upstairs. She wasn't sure why she was on tip-toes, Mrs Madison wouldn't hear anything from the kitchen and besides, she was perfectly entitled to be climbing the stairs in the house she was a guest in. It just felt like she should.

The corridor which the study and Richard's bedroom were on was one of two that led off from the wider one where she had her room. She stopped quickly in her own room to pick up her clutch bag, just in case she needed to conceal anything she might be inspired to 'borrow' as evidence.

This far into the house she felt more confident of her step and broke into a brisk trot, keen to get this over with as quickly as possible. Richard's door was closed. She knew he wasn't in the house, let alone his bedroom, but she still felt a sharp tang of nerves as she walked past the spot where the creaky floorboard had nearly been her undoing the night before. She pulled out a hairpin and set to work on the lock again.

The room was a lot easier to navigate in daylight, and she could see there was some semblance of order to the chaos she'd experienced in the half-light of the dim bulb. Shelves were all carefully numbered and labelled, alphabetical order and dates all correct and precise. Richard's father certainly didn't seem to have been the kind of man who would leave his estate without the certainty of a will, she thought. The chair she'd used as a ladder was pushed back in place, and she quickly pulled it back out again, placing a thick hard-back book on the seat to give herself the necessary extra height. Standing carefully, one hand against the wall-shelves to steady the wobbling, she reached up and pulled down the red-leather case. It was locked too, but no problem to her.

She cleared a space on the cluttered desk then went to work with her hairpin again, before flipping open the lid. Inside she saw a bundle of letters addressed to Lord Melmersby. Some were stamped with a red triangle and the words *"Passed Censor"* or with markings that said *"Field Post Office"*. Letters from the trenches. None of them had been opened.

Below the bundle was a name tag – a dark red circle of hard fibre, stamped with letters and numbers that meant nothing to Ellie, but for one set across the top: *"Cpt BBA Lindley"*. She felt her heart hammer against the inside of her chest. At the bottom of the case, a torn piece of cloth, grey-green in the most part, but stained dark in places. She lifted it up to inspect more closely, and there below it she saw two more envelopes, unmarked and unsealed. She pushed open the first. Inside were three feathers, almost identical to each other. Each pure white. No words, just feathers. She carefully placed it back and took up the other envelope. Inside this one, a scrap of paper folded in two. As she unfolded it something fell out onto the desk. On the paper was a single word, scrawled and misspelt as if a child had written it: *"COWERD"*. Looking down to where the object had fallen from it, she saw it settled on the desk, bigger and rougher than the others but unmistakably the same message: a single white feather.

"No! There's another one!" she called out loud to herself.

"What in the name of God are you doing in my study, Miss Blaine?"

Ellie span around, dropping the letter, to see Richard Lindley standing in the doorway of the study, an iron poker in his hand. She frantically looked back at the window, but it had been nailed shut since she made her escape through that way last night.

"I–" she started.

"What have you got there? Good Lord! That is my private property. How dare you. How dare you!" Richard stepped forward, the poker still in his hand, and Ellie grabbed an ivory-handled letter opener that lay on the edge of the desk.

"I might be small, but I put up a fight!" she said, holding the letter opener in front of her.

Richard stared at her, then looked at the poker in his hand, shaking his head before throwing it onto the top of a short stack of shelves with a clatter.

"I got back early and saw the door ajar – I thought there'd been another break-in," he said, his voice calmer now. "Well there has been – only I didn't expect it to be you. What on earth possessed you–?" he looked at the feather on the desk, and the fallen letter. "Ah, I see. You think I'm the killer? Is that it?"

Ellie shook her head, unconvincingly.

"You think I murdered Malkie and Vivienne in revenge for some terrible slight. Is that what you think?"

"No," Ellie said, even more unconvincingly. "And Dr Waterman?" she added, nervously.

"What?" Richard said, then closed his eyes and shook his head again. "Yes, and Dr Waterman. I suppose you think I murdered him too?"

"Who's the fourth one?" Ellie said, still looking carefully for a way out that didn't take her too close to Richard.

"The fourth? Oh, the feathers you mean," Richard said, suddenly sensing Ellie's nerves and stepping back to give her more room. "No idea. It was left for me in my bedroom when I came back home for Bertie's funeral. Whoever did it disguised the writing, I'm sure, so I wouldn't tell. Which is ironic, for someone accusing a fellow of cowardice."

"Why did you lie to me?" Ellie said suddenly, and Richard pulled his head back sharply and narrowed his eyes.

"Lie to you? About what, exactly?"

Ellie cleared her throat. "You told me you fought with Bertie, that you were there when he died. But you were given these feathers because you refused to sign up. So why did you lie about being with Bertie?"

Richard let out a long sigh. "I didn't lie to you. I said I was with Bertie, I didn't at any point say I was there to fight." He stepped back suddenly out of the room, clearing the way for Ellie and gesturing with his hand that she should take it.

"You know," he said as she nervously eyed the space he'd left for her to pass, "when Bertie told me he had met an American girl and fallen in love with her, we all thought he was a dizzy fool. He was prepared to give up any hopes he had of an advantageous marriage all because he'd had his head turned by some pretty little Yankee cheesecake—"

"Hey, now wait a minute—" Ellie started.

"But you know, I listened to him, and how he spoke of you and I came to realise he really was deeply in love with you, and so for a moment I was happy for him and I stood up for him, and for you, in the face of mother and father's strong disapproval. But here you are, and it turns out you are exactly as I suspected you would be: an impetuous, hot-headed, over-confident, brash American woman who doesn't know her place!"

"Excuse me?" Ellie said, suddenly tempted to pick up the letter opener again.

"Well, I do know your place," Richard continued, "and it damn well isn't here! If you want to believe I'm a killer and a coward – and God knows you won't be the first – then I can only assume you would want nothing to do with me, nor be welcoming of my hospitality. I have some work to attend to with Dr Waterman's patients until the end of the week, then I shall personally escort you back to Southampton and see that you get a ticket back on the next ship to the United States."

Ellie was silent, caught somewhere between anger at his words and guilt at her actions in breaking into his study. She slipped silently past him and walked down the corridor, back in the direction of her own room, feeling his hard stare burn into the back of her neck as she walked.

Was he the killer? If he was, he put on a good show of brazening it out. If he was, she wasn't sure she felt safe travelling to Southampton with him, nor even spending another night in the house. And if he wasn't? Then she might be even keener to leave, rather than have to face him over breakfast again after everything she'd done.

She could do no more digging around at Melmersby Hall, that was sure. She still had questions, but she was no longer sure where to go to find the answers.

ELLIE BLAINE 1920s MYSTERIES

CHAPTER 18

SHE was alive. That was the first thing she noticed when she woke up, still early enough that the sun hadn't risen to spill its light through the cracks of her bedroom blind. That was something, she thought; she hadn't been murdered in her sleep at least. But she didn't yet feel safe enough – from danger or embarrassment – to go down to breakfast before Richard left the house. She was relieved to hear the sound of his car pulling off along the gravel drive just a few minutes after she'd woken, but she still waited until well after the sun had risen to get up and put on her day clothes. She stepped nervously down the stairs to find Georgie sitting in the lounge reading a copy of The Times and puffing on a pipe.

"Georgie, am I glad you are back! I didn't know you smoked?" Ellie said, sitting down on the opposite sofa.

"Mmm" Georgie mumbled, pulling the pipe out of her mouth. "Good morning. I don't usually, just on special occasions."

"What's the occasion?"

"I've had to…" Georgie's words were suddenly swallowed by a sharp fit of coughing, and she had to wipe her eyes with the sleeve of her jacket before continuing. "I have just attended my last ghastly dinner of the year at the Inns of Court."

"Dinner?"

Georgie tapped out the contents of her pipe into a crystal ashtray balanced on the chair arm. "Yes – medieval nonsense. You have to eat a certain amount of dinners with all the other fellows hoping to make a go of it in law. Most of them are crashing bores; or else they are either horrified by, or a little too keen on, having a woman, of all creatures, dining with them. Terrible waste of a trip to London. So what's been going on while I've been away?"

Ellie hesitated for a moment. "I don't know if you heard, but Dr Waterman is missing, and the police think—"

"Oh yes," Georgie said suddenly, "Richard told me, dreadful business, absolutely dreadful."

Ellie nodded then turned to look out of the window towards the driveway that led out of Melmersby Hall.

"I may leave," she said quietly.

"Leave?" Georgie said, sitting up sharply. "Leave here? Why? When?"

Ellie turned back, smiling sadly at her friend. "Today. Before Richard gets back. I feel I may have outstayed my welcome."

"Well you can't leave," Georgie said, standing up now and striding up to Ellie to take a firm hold of both her arms. "You absolutely can't. I won't allow it, and besides you can't walk to York and there are no buses running today and I can't drive so you are stuck here with me and you shall jolly well enjoy it!"

Ellie laughed and shook her head. "I guess I'm stuck then. I just wish…" Ellie's voice faded as she looked again out of the window, across to the entrance to Malkie's garage. The door had been left open, and she could see no-one had yet tidied up the bits and pieces the unfortunate chauffeur had left there: his torch, the car jack, his lunchbox.

"Yes?" Georgie said, tilting her head to throw Ellie a curious look. "Wish what?"

"Do you know what?" Ellie said, turning sharply to face her friend. "I think I shall stay a little longer. Do you fancy a little trip?"

"Trip?' Georgie said, clasping her hands together. "Absolutely! Anywhere exciting?"

"That depends what we find there," Ellie said. "I think I might have been looking in the wrong place."

* * *

"Well it's a little less exciting than I was hoping," Georgie said wistfully as they pulled up outside a small, stone cottage with an even smaller, but neatly kept, front garden of spring flowers and early English roses.

They'd taken two of the bicycles that were stored in the smaller garage to the side of the Hall and cycled the short three miles to Cowthorpe, a hamlet just the other side of the hill that marked the boundary of Lord Melmersby's land.

"So tell me again what you're hoping to find here?" Georgie said.

"I told you," Ellie said, pushing open the small wooden garden gate, "answers."

"Yes," Georgie said, following in gingerly behind as the gate snapped back on its tight spring, nearly catching her leg, "it's just, I'm still not sure of the questions."

Ellie rapped hard on the grey-painted wooden door. "Well hopefully you'll be clearer in a minute, if she's in. Ah – here she is."

At the sound of a latch being pulled, Ellie stepped back to allow the door to swing open and reveal a short, slightly stooped woman dressed in a black housecoat and holding a cup of tea in one hand. "Can I help you?" the woman said cautiously.

"Mrs Fawthrop, I'm real sorry to bother you, but I was hoping I might talk to you about your late husband. I think I might be able to help get to the bottom of what happened to him."

***

"Would you like another cuppa?" Widow Fawthrop seemed determined that neither Ellie nor Georgie would leave the house without trying every one of the multitude of teas she kept in a miscellany of pots that filled the shelves of her tiny kitchen. "This one's a favourite of Malkie's, from Berinag, I think it says on my label, right up in the high Himalanias – he picked it up when he was in India, it's very refreshing."

"How long ago was he in India, Mrs Fawthrop?" Ellie said, taking a sip of the dark, green brew.

"1896, he came back the last time. Yes, that would be right, because James – that's our second son – he was born in '97."

Ellie put the teacup carefully back in its saucer, wondering if there might be a convenient pot plant that needed watering nearby. "Lovely," she said.

"So," Mrs Fawthrop said, putting a hand on Georgie's leg, which she'd crossed in order to fit into the tiny wooden kitchen chair she'd been given to relax in. "You've heard enough about me, what is it exactly that you wanted to ask me about?"

Ellie glanced up at the clock above the fireplace. They'd been here nearly 40 minutes and she'd not asked her first question yet. Not that she minded, however old the tea was; it would be a tough question for Widow Fawthrop and she was happy to wait until she was comfortable to answer.

"I believe your husband had something, Mrs Fawthrop, something that the old Lord Melmersby gave him? A promissory letter, or a document of some kind – to do with an inheritance?"

Mrs Fawthrop shook her head and Ellie thought she could see a shiver run through her. "That blessed thing, I wish he'd never had it," she said.

"So you know about it?" Georgie said, suddenly excited that the whole trip wasn't to just be tea-tasting in an ill-fitting chair.

"Aye, I do," she said. "But don't you go saying nothing to the police about it, they are bound to get the wrong end of the stick and I just can't be doing with that fuss."

"I won't," Ellie said. "It'll just be between you and me. So there was something?"

"Malkie was a great favourite of Lord Melmersby, he was," Widow Fawthrop said, suddenly putting down her tea. "Trusted him like no other. My Malkie, he said to me: 'Lord Melmersby trusts me with his most important business'. That's what he told me. Said his lordship told him things about his private dealings and whatnot and that he would never tell them to another living soul, not even me, his own wife."

"I see," Ellie said. "And you have no idea what these business matters were?"

Mrs Fawthrop shook her head. "No. He was a good secret keeper, my Malkie. I'll give him that. Anyhow, Lord Melmersby must have liked him as he left him a good deal when he died. Gave him a promise, all sealed and signed for and official like."

"A good deal?" Ellie said. "And what happened?"

Mrs Fawthrop's face flushed deep red. "Well, a good deal to the likes of us, probably not for his lordship, mind. Still, it was a lot for us."

"So he didn't leave Malkie the whole estate?" Georgie said, her voice rising in excitement.

Mrs Fawthrop laughed. "Oh my dear, no! Why would he do that? No, it was just something he left him for some work that Malkie did for him years ago, he said. That's all I know. As for what happened to it..." Her voice faded out.

"And the document went missing? Do you think someone stole it?" Ellie asked.

"Well I suppose if you put it like that, yes," Mrs Fawthrop said quietly.

"Did Malkie think it was Dr Lindley who took the document? Might your husband have tried to take it back?"

Mrs Fawthrop nodded, then suddenly sat up. "I hope you don't think my Malkie was the one what broke in and took that cup and whatnot. He was sat here with me all that night, helping me soak my bunions. Besides, with his lumbago he could barely get up the stairs, never mind climb up the side of Melmersby Hall. That weren't him."

Ellie nodded. "I'm sure it wasn't. But do you know who might have taken the document?"

Mrs Fawthrop's head dropped. "I do, yes."

"And?" Georgie said, uncrossing her legs to lean forward in anticipation.

"It were me," Mrs Fawthrop said, her head dropping further until she was staring at her own slippered-feet.

"You?" Ellie exclaimed. "But why?"

She lifted her head again. "You're from America aren't you, Miss Blaine?"

"I am," she said, confused.

"Well, I am sure America is a lovely place. My Malkie certainly thought so. He loved all them new moving pictures what they show at Harrogate, and he talked about New York, and the buildings there that touch the sky, and the West and all the wide open spaces and all the land just waiting for those what will go and get it. If he'd got his hands on that money, well, he'd have been gone, you see. He'd have been gone off to America to follow his dream, so he said. Only I'd have not gone with him. Not as he didn't want me to go, but I love it here in Yorkshire. This is where I was born and this is where I intend to die, and be buried next my nana and my grandpa and my dear old mum and dad in the churchyard in Melmersby. So he thought that bit of paper was a blessing, you see. But I thought it was a curse. 'Cos either he'd leave me here all on my own, or else I'd be the one to stop his dream and he'd blame me until the day he died, even if he would never say as much. So I took care of it. It ain't in Melmersby Hall, nor anywhere else, c'ept up that there chimney in smoke and ash. And now my poor Malkie is in the churchyard waiting for me, and I may as well tell you all I've done as I shall have to reckon it up with him when I join him."

Mrs Fawthrop sank her head down again, sobbing and wiping her face on her apron. Ellie put a comforting arm to her, while Georgie offered her the still-full cup of decades-old Indian tea she was holding.

"It might help?" she said, hopefully.

***

After a good hour more of tea and sympathy, while Mrs Fawthrop pulled herself together enough to brew up another pot of tea – this time, to Ellie's relief, a fresh batch from Harrogate – they left her to her memories and walked back to where they'd left the bikes.

"So, it wasn't Malkie breaking into Melmersby Hall," Ellie said.

"And it wasn't Richard trying to stop him inheriting the Hall," Georgie said, raising an admonishing eyebrow.

"I suppose not," Ellie said, picking up the handlebar of her bike. "So who was it that dropped the car on him? And why?"

"Richard told me about the feathers you found," Georgie said, scanning Ellie for a reaction.

"Did he? I suppose he told you I made a complete fool of myself, breaking into his study and accusing him of lying about his war record?"

"Oh yes, and he used those exact words if I recall," Georgie said with a mischievous grin. "And a few other choice ones besides. You know he joined the RAMC, the Medical Corps? Those chaps might not have fought but they did some of the most dangerous work in the whole war, clearing the wounded out of shell holes under enemy fire and such. Those feathers were ridiculous. People can be so cruel, and stupid; even those who should know better. Richard has many flaws, and don't I know it. But cowardice was certainly never one of them."

"Well, yes, I can see that. But then you are absolutely sure Richard can't be the killer? I don't see that anyone else had a motive."

"Well, that is a mystery," Georgie said, as she swung her leg over the bike frame and tested the pedal. "But I'm sure Inspector Blaine is working on it right now, am I right?"

Ellie laughed. "Well, I'm not going to stop now am I?" She pushed off suddenly with her heels and the bike was away up the gentle slope out of Cowthorpe.

"Race you to Melmersby," she called out, pedalling faster still. "Last one there has to drink another cup of tea!"

CHAPTER 19

"WE'RE taking a detour!" Ellie called out as they crested the top of Cowthorpe Hill.

"You're just changing the rules because I caught you up," Georgie wheezed, standing upright on the pedals to squeeze her bike up the last few yards of the slope.

"We're going downhill now, you'll be pleased to hear," Ellie said, looking at her friend's increasingly bright pink face – forehead beaded with perspiration. "But not to Melmersby Hall, not yet. There's someone we need to talk to in the village."

Georgie puffed out her cheeks as she wobbled her bike to a halt alongside Ellie at the top of the hill. To the left, the road continued along to the back of the Hall; to the right, it cut back down steeply to join the village at the bridge end. "And who might that be?" she asked.

"Malkie kept secrets," Ellie said, turning her bike to face the steep right-hand slope. "That's what his wife said. And I've learned from you that there's only one place to go in Melmersby if you want to find out people's secrets. Fancy another cup of tea?"

"Not really!" Georgie called out as Ellie suddenly pushed off to head rapidly down the winding road.

"You can have a coffee!" she called back, before disappearing around a steep bend.

* * *

"Now you ladies must be hungry after your bike ride?" Mrs Garnet looked sympathetically at Georgie's pink-blushed face: "And you, dear, look like you need a lie-down and a nice cup of lapsang souchong."

"Some carrot cake would be nice," Georgie said, dropping heavily into a straight-backed wooden chair. "And I don't suppose you serve whisky, do you?"

Mrs Garnet raised her eyes. "I shall bring you some cake. I made it myself this morning, you won't get better in the village."

"This is the only Tea Shoppe in the village, so that's not saying much," Georgie said, under her breath and just quietly enough that Mrs Garnet wouldn't hear it as she nipped back through the beaded curtain to the kitchen.

"Play nice with her," Ellie said. "We need her in a good mood – and you know she hears everything."

"I heard Dr Lindley say just the same thing the other day, Mrs Garnet," Ellie called out.

Mrs Garnet's angular face popped out from between the strands of the curtain. "Eh? He said what?"

"That he'd never tasted better carrot cake in his life. He said it was much better than any he'd tasted in London – even at the Ritz."

"He said that, did he?" The whole of Mrs Garnet was now out from behind the curtain, and her face was stretched in a broad grin.

"He did, I heard him too," Georgie said, suddenly catching on. "He said it was even better than the one they serve at Betty's in Harrogate."

Mrs Garnet was now out from behind the counter entirely, and standing over the table where the two women nodded confirmation to each other that that was exactly what they'd heard.

"Betty's? The new Tea Shop everyone is talking about?" she asked, tugging at the string of her apron to straighten it up.

"The very same," Georgie said. "In fact, Richard said their carrot cake tasted like the scrapings from the bottom of a compost pile compared to– ouch!"

"Oh, I'm sorry Georgie, was that your foot?" Ellie said, raising her eyebrow enough to let

Georgie know this particular cake didn't need another cherry on top. "Anyway, Mrs Garnet, it seems people just can't get enough of your delicious baking."

Mrs Garnet shook her head. "Well, perhaps you should tell them to come in here a bit more often to buy it," she said. "It's been terribly quiet here these last few weeks."

"We were just visiting Widow Fawthrop," Ellie said. "She was saying she must come over and try some soon. Apparently, she would have come more often but her late husband didn't like her coming here."

Mrs Garnet pulled her head back so far that her chin appeared to disappear into her neck. "Didn't like…why he never…why on earth would she say such a thing?"

"Yes, why?" Georgie said, looking equally puzzled for a moment then quickly correcting herself. "Why… did she say that…thing she said, when we were both there. Sitting in her living room."

Ellie shrugged. "He seemed to think that there was gossip about him, and that it… well, I said it can't possibly be, but he seemed to think it originated here."

"Here? Why, the very nerve of the man!" Mrs Garnet's face was turning as pink as the icing on her cherry bakewells, and she turned with a theatrical twirl towards the kitchen, then sharply back again to address the two women.

"If there's gossip, it won't have started here. And if there is, well – he's only got himself to blame, hasn't he. With all the carry on and what not, it's no wonder some people talk."

Ellie winked at Georgie, who shook her head with a subtle smile. "I was only saying to Georgie on the way over, I'm sure if there was gossip in the village, there must have been good reason for it."

"Reason? Oh mark my words there was reason alright. Carrying on with that… that woman, and his poor wife just recently with child. Shameful, that's what it was."

Ellie pulled her seat closer to the table as Mrs Garnet sat down next to them. "So, this would have been a while ago, then? Nothing recent?"

Mrs Garnet shook her head. "People would say, Malkie and Lily Fawthrop, they were as devoted as Jack and Jill. But some of us knew better." She sat herself down at Ellie and Georgie's table, folding her arms firmly as she leaned in towards them. "You wouldn't think it now, but back then Malkie was quite the fine-looking man. Been in the army you see, held himself with military bearing, very straight and proper. Or so folk thought."

"So he was seeing someone? A woman?"

"A Jesobel, if you ask me. Carrying on with a married man and his wife expecting."

"Was this someone in the village?"

Mrs Garnet puffed out her chest. "She lived over Brayford way. Worked at the Hall for a short while, chambermaid I believe. It seems Mr

Fawthrop took a shine to her while she were there. Got in the habit of paying her visits he did, at all times of the night. He might have thought he could keep it all under wraps, what with it being carried on over the valley top, but people come a long way for my baking and people talk. He'd turn up in the middle of the night, or the early morning – bold as brass, and using Lord Melmersby's car like it was own. The cheek of it."

"And what happened? Did he get caught?"

Mrs Garnet huffed deeply. "Did he 'eck. The devil takes care of his own, I say. His poor wife never did find out. And I never told a soul, despite what her husband had to say. Well, not many souls anyway. Only those as I trust, like."

Ellie nodded seriously. "Well, I'm glad you trust us. Do you know what happened to the woman?"

She shrugged. "One day she just packed up and left, they say. No-one knows where she went – I heard folk say she went to Harrogate, and some said she went over Glossop way. There was rumours she had a husband in the Navy what came back, or that she got consumption, or all sorts. Anyway, she left and Malkie went back to playing the faithful husband with his new baby boy as if nothing had happened. Now, I won't have folk saying I gossip, so don't you go breathing a word of this to no-one."

" Absolutely," Ellie said. "Our lips are sealed."

"We shall be every bit as discreet as you, of course," Georgie added. "Could I possibly try that carrot cake now?"

* * *

The ride back from the village to the Hall was flat and leisurely and fueled by tea and cake. They put the bikes back into the smaller garage and Georgie groaned as she stretched out her back.

"I'm really not used to being quite so energetic. I believe I may have become decadent since I started spending more time in London," she said. "I shall endeavour to get back to being a proper Yorkshire lady and ride out more often."

Ellie laughed. "I'm sure Richard can give you a lift home once he gets back." Her smile faded at the thought of his return. She didn't have much to get ready, but she would need to think about packing if he was to follow through with his promise to take her back to Southampton. She'd miss Georgie, that much was clear. But now she thought she might miss Melmersby a little too, even the Hall.

"Everything all right, Ellie?" Georgie said.

"Yes," she said, snapping suddenly out of her thoughts. "Let's get inside, I'm sure a scotch on the rocks will sort you out."

Georgie's expression suggested she agreed, and the two of them linked arms as they crunched through the pea-shingle path that led around to the entrance of the house. On the broad driveway ahead, a black, hard-topped car was parked at an awkward angle

"Who's is that?" Ellie asked.

Georgie put her hands on her hips. "I do believe it's our favourite Detective Inspector. I wonder what he's doing here now?"

CHAPTER 20

"ARCHIE, I didn't expect to see you. How are you doing with yourself, you must be going through the most trying time?"

It seemed DI Lochner wasn't the only unexpected guest in the house. The table had been pulled out in the drawing room and Archie's hard-backed chair was pushed in so close his chin almost touched the table edge as he slouched down in it.

"Well, Georgie old girl," he said, ever-so-slightly sitting up as he saw the two new arrivals, "it has been difficult. I was just telling the sergeant here–"

"Detective Inspector," DI Lochner said firmly, without looking up from the notepad he was scribbling in."

"I was just telling the inspector here, it's been quite the rum go. Her family are taking care of all the arrangements and whatnot. Three years we were married, part of their family and all that; and not a word from any of them to ask how I am. The only communication I've had was from that wretched brother of hers sending his man around to take his car back. Well, he didn't waste any time did he? It's quite trying, I won't lie to you."

"Well, I'm sure you'll have the chance to talk things through with them after the funeral. I'm sure they are just very upset," Georgie said, taking a seat on the opposite side of the table to him. "If you like, I shall keep you company there."

Archie shuffled a little in his seat, pulling himself up enough to put his elbows on the table. "Well, that's the thing. I shan't be at the funeral. I thought it best, you know, what with how they are with me and all that. The thing is, they jolly well think I did it! Can you believe that? They think I bumped dear old Viv off myself!"

DI Lochner finally looked up from his notebook. "If we could continue, Mr Beauclère: I should like to know when and where your wife came into possession of a hip flask of whisky?" The inspector gestured to Ellie to take a seat, keeping his gaze on Archie as he did.

"Good Lord, I've told you and your constable this a dozen times now! She always carries... carried a little something to perk herself up, especially at social events. She could be quite sour without it. To be honest, she could be quite sour with it." He looked toward Georgie, perhaps hoping for more than the frown he got back.

"And she filled this flask at home – your home – you say? Before you arrived at Melmersby Hall for the service?"

"Well yes, of course. She wanted something to help her through the service, you see, for old Lord Melmersby."

DI Lochner scratched something down in his notebook. "And was it ever out of her sight, during this time?"

Archie shrugged. "I suppose she put it down before we went to dinner. It's rather hard to hide a flask when you are in an evening dress, and besides there was plenty to drink on the table."

The inspector looked up again, this time glancing around all three table guests to make sure he had their attention. "And yet, when she was discovered in this very room, bereft of life, the flask was beside her, and it appeared to contain a high concentration of chloral hydrate. Could you explain that?"

Archie pulled in his chin, grimacing. "Well, no. I'm quite stumped about that."

"And it was you, Mr Beauclère, who discovered her body in the drawing room?" DI Lochner turned to address Ellie and Georgie. "Did anyone witness any other person or persons attending to Mrs Beauclère between the time she was escorted from the table and the discovery of her body?"

"Now hold on!" Archie was suddenly sitting bolt upright. "I can see where this is going and it's not on, I tell you, it's really not. We all know whoever bumped off my dear wife was the same fellow who did for Malkie Fawthrop, and now Simon, you tell me – it was the mad feather killer! That's where you should be looking, not making wild accusations at the bereaved husband."

The inspector coughed. "No-one is making accusations, Mr Beauclère. Could you tell me what you know about Dr Waterman's disappearance? You mentioned a feather?"

Archie threw his hands out wide and looked pleadingly at Ellie and Georgie. "Oh come on! Everyone knows about that by now. He got the same feather as the other two and next thing you know his car is found abandoned up at Cowthorpe top and no sign of the fellow anywhere. So he's either been bumped off by the same devil who killed my dear wife or else topped himself out of fear. I thought you were supposed to be a detective, Mr Lochner? There's your modus operandi or whatnot – you should be out looking for some deranged lunatic with a penchant for chickens!"

"That will be all for now, Mr Beauclère," DI Lochner said, purposefully closing his notebook and rising from the table. "If one of you would be so good as to tell Dr Lindley that I came calling for him, that would be most appreciated. I shall call again at a more convenient time. Thank you for your cooperation, Mr Beauclère. Good day to you."

Archie folded his arms and shook his head as the inspector picked up his hat from the table and went to leave.

"I'll see you to the door," Ellie said, standing.

"Thank you, Miss Blaine."

Ellie showed the inspector through the door to the entrance hall, following on behind. "Were you looking for Richard?" she said, as she handed him his coat from the stand by the outer door.

"I was, miss," he said, with a nod of thanks for his raincoat. "It wasn't a wasted trip though. I had questions for Mr Beauclère too, so that has saved me some valuable time."

"Are you any closer to finding the killer?" Ellie asked. From the inspector's expression, she thought perhaps her tone might have given away more of her ambitions in the case than she meant to.

"We have a few promising lines of inquiry," he said, looking at her through narrowed eyes. "If you have any information you feel might be relevant, please do make sure you bring it to our attention as soon as possible. We're dealing with someone who has already taken lives, Miss Blaine. This is a job for the professionals."

Ellie felt her smile was probably no more convincing than the tone of her voice, but she tried it anyway. "Absolutely," she said. "If I hear anything, you shall be the first to know."

DI Lochner eyed Ellie suspiciously, then raised his hat and disappeared out into the early afternoon air, as she returned to the drawing room to find

Archie now slumped back almost perpendicular to the floor.

"The nerve of the chap," he said, waving his hand dismissively in the direction of the door. "I'm in mourning, I shouldn't have to put up with…"

"Would you like a drink?" Ellie said, casually popping open the stopper of a crystal decanter that stood on the dresser. "I take it you aren't driving, what with your brother-in-law taking back the car?"

"What? Oh, yes. That's right. A drink would be splendid, my nerves are shot with all that heavy-handed interrogation. Thank you."

Archie took the tumbler and Ellie offered another to Georgie, who shook her head, then sat down again at the table. "How did you get here, Archie? We passed through Brackley the other day, it's quite a way from here, without a car."

He drew a deep gulp from the glass, inspecting it to see if there was any left, before putting it down slowly. "Um, yes. I had to catch the wretched bus. I suppose I should get used to that, what?" He looked around for sympathy that wasn't there. "I say, does anyone mind if I light up a cigarette?"

Ellie shook her head and Georgie shrugged as Archie fumbled for his silver cigarette holder, offering them around before picking up his lighter from the table and flicking it to life to light one up and draw deeply on it.

"I might just pop in and see Mrs Madison," Ellie said, standing up again. "Maybe she could rustle something up for a snack. I'm quite peckish."

"I'm still quite full from all that cake," Georgie said. "I'm surprised you've got room for anything yourself – you had more than me."

Ellie smiled. "The bike ride has given me an appetite."

Georgie nodded and stood up to join her friend. "Bye Archie, nice to see you again."

Archie puffed out a great cloud of smoke. "Oh, I'm staying. I shall be here until Richard gets back. I shall amuse myself somehow, don't you mind me."

Georgie patted him on the shoulder then hurried to catch up to her friend.

"It's ok Georgie, you stay and keep Archie company for a bit longer. I shan't be long."

Georgie narrowed her eyes suspiciously. "What are you up to? If you're playing private detective again then I absolutely insist on being your stuffy but reliable sidekick."

Ellie laughed. "I can't imagine you being anyone's sidekick, Georgie, particularly not a stuffy one. But I really think you should sit this one out, I won't be a minute."

Georgie shrugged, her expression a mix of curiosity and disappointment. "Very well, but whatever you are up to, I should be the first one to know what you find out."

"You will be,' Ellie said, patting her friend on the arm and turning to flip the latch of the white, wooden kitchen door.

As Ellie opened, Mrs Madison was sat in a sturdy kitchen chair with a tea cloth draped over her face, snoring loudly. Mr Madison, who was curled up across her lap, looked up, turned a lip, then jumped grumpily down to disappear behind the door to the pantry that stood slightly ajar. Mrs Madison snorted loudly, then sat up with a start, pulling the cloth from over her eyes.

"Oh my, yes, well… here we are… good afternoon. Yes. I was just resting my eyes. Onions, you see. Chopping onions."

"Good afternoon, Mrs Madison," Ellie said, picking up the tea cloth from the floor and handing it back to the housekeeper. "I was just wondering if Lucy was around, I was wanting to ask her advice on what to wear for my journey back to Southampton."

Mrs Madison now sat up even more sharply, and Ellie could swear she saw her eyes brighten. "Oh, you're leaving, Miss Blaine? When do you leave? I shall be more than happy to help you pack and on your way."

"I'm sure you would be," Ellie said dryly. "I believe I shall be on my way tomorrow, I'll arrange it with Richard when he returns this afternoon. I was hoping to catch Lucy before I go, to say thank you for all her help."

"Well, I believe she has gone over to Jim's house, with her usual little comfort parcel," Mrs Madison said. "She's a good girl like that."

"Well," Ellie said, smiling. "I'm sure that's just a reflection on her upbringing. You've have done a wonderful job of raising her."

Mrs Madison stood fully now, the faintest flush of pink on her round cheeks as she patted down her apron. "Well, yes. I done my best by the girl. I am firm with her at times, it is true, but my own mother said 'spare the rod, spoil the child,' and I would say Lucy can be a little wild at times, but there's no one can say she's been spoiled."

"Of course," Ellie said, gently re-arranging some drying flowers that sat in a vase on the kitchen dresser. "Her mother must have been a good friend, for you to take such good care of Lucy for her."

"Well," Mrs Madison hesitated. "I done my best, like I said."

"What happened to her mother?" Ellie said, dropping the stem of a withered pink rose back into the narrow vase neck.

Mrs Madison frowned at the question. "She didn't survive having her daughter, poor thing."

"I suppose she's buried in the churchyard here?" Ellie said, "I should like to put some flowers on her grave – just as a gesture. For Lucy."

"No," Mrs Madison said, the pink in her face deepening. "She's not. She wasn't local, see. Anyhow, can't sit here yacking, I've got work to do."

"Oh, perhaps I should go over Brayford way? I believe there's a churchyard there?"

Mrs Madison's face had now turned a deeper pink than the dried rose. "Why would you… I really don't… whatever do you mean?"

"I'm sure Richard could drop me off, to pay my respects, on my way back."

Mrs Madison fidgeted uneasily in her chair. "Well, you see, the thing is; buried in a pauper's grave you see, poor thing. Unmarked. That's as I've told Lucy, no-one really knows…"

"You didn't really know her mother, did you?" Ellie said, suddenly dropping the warm tone from her voice.

"I don't know what you are talking about. Have you been listening to village gossip? You shouldn't believe a word of it," Mrs Madison's voice was rising higher with each word and she frantically looked around her feet for any sign of Mr Madison, perhaps hoping he might back her up.

"I'm leaving tomorrow, Mrs Madison," Ellie said. "I shall be away back in Indiana, never to darken your kitchen doorstep again. You can tell me. I won't say a word. Or perhaps I could ask Richard what he knows about it?"

The housekeeper slumped back into her chair, her arms dropping into her lap, palms open in resignation. "No," Mrs Madison said, her head bowed. "I didn't know her." She looked up again, fire suddenly back in her droopy eyes. "Do you think I might have a little of my pick-me-up cordial?"

Ellie nodded and took the bottle from the shelf to hand to Mrs Madison, who pulled the cork with her teeth and took a deep swallow.

"I can't lie. Not no more. Don't you go saying nothing to Lucy, mind. She doesn't know a thing. If she finds out I was fibbing all these years–"

"Was it Malkie?" Ellie said. "Who brought you the baby?"

The housekeeper nodded. "I've kept this secret so long now, but he's gone so I suppose it's time to let it go. Told me he'd found the girl abandoned by the roadside, that's what he said. Said I was not to breathe a word to anyone. Course I knew that weren't the truth. Would have broken poor Lily's heart. But I couldn't let that little baby suffer for the sins of her parents. And he paid me well. Only for her upkeep, of course, I didn't make a penny from it." She stressed the last words firmly.

"I'm sure you did what you could for Lucy," Ellie said.

Mrs Madison's face was whiter than her apron now. "Please, promise me, not a word. If... oh Mr Madison! What have you got there? Take him out you naughty man!"

Mr Madison had waddled out from under the table with an air of satisfaction, his mouth full of the grey, twitching fur of a terrified mouse. He dropped the injured beast to the floor and began to poke at its trembling body to get it to move again.

"Give me that!" Mrs Madison said firmly. "You're nothing but trouble! Naughty Mr Madison!"

The cat put down his ears while Mrs Madison scooped up the unfortunate mouse by its tail, holding it gingerly in one hand while opening the kitchen window with the other to fling the poor creature to its fate in the herb garden. "Horrible things, mice," she said, running her hand under the cold tap.

"Poor mouse," Ellie said, grimacing. "We have a cat at home and he's always bringing little things in like that. I just wish they'd finish them off, it always seems a bit cruel the way they play with their food."

Mrs Madison shook her head vigorously. "Oh no, that's just their way. He's not playing. A mouse might not look much to you, but if you're the size of Mr Madison they'll give you a right nasty nip. He just has to soften them a bit before he gets close in to finish them off. Self-preservation, that's what they call it."

Ellie looked down quizzically at Mr Madison, who was now grumpily biting at his own claws, scanning the room for any trace of his lost prize. He didn't look like a cat who needed to worry about his lunch putting up a fight.

"Anyway," Ellie said, shaking her head at Mr Madison's undignified attempt at cleaning his round, threadbare belly while squatting on his own tail. "Thank you for being honest. I shall take the secret back with me to—"

"Ellie, Mrs Madison, so sorry to interrupt." The door had swung open and Georgie now stepped into the kitchen, her face a picture of concern.

"That's perfectly fine, Miss Georgina," Mrs Madison said, quickly replacing the expression of concern on her face for a broad grin that did little to disguise the hot flush of her cheeks. "We were just… swapping cake recipes."

"Really?" Georgie said, raising an eyebrow and looking between the two women then shaking her head. "Well, I'm sure whatever you're cooking up will be fascinating, but we have a visitor: Rev Barton, and he appears a little upset."

"Oh my," Mrs Madison said. "The vicar is here and look at the state of me. I've not even got my proper shoes on, and my hair…"

"We'll take care of this," Ellie said, smiling. "You put your feet up, Mrs Madison. Maybe have another little drop of your pick-me-up cordial, I think you've earned it. Thank you so much."

"Must have been a very good recipe," Georgie said slyly, as Ellie stepped past her through the door.

Ellie winked at her. "It was."

ELLIE BLAINE 1920s MYSTERIES

CHAPTER 21

"AH, hello, yes." Rev Barton's cheeks glowed soft pink as Ellie walked into the drawing room where he was nervously pacing the floor. His double chin sank down so low as he spoke that it almost covered his dog collar. "Miss Blaine. Before I say anything; about that unfortunate 'sales girl' remark, I…"

"It's not a problem," Ellie said, waving away his concern. "How can we help you?"

The vicar's ferret-like eyes darted around the room. "I was rather hoping Lord Melmersby would be here, there's a concerning matter…"

"Richard will be back shortly," Georgie said. "Perhaps you could wait with Archie there?"

The vicar glanced over to the sofa where Archie raised a weak wave, shaking circles in the haze of smoke that hung around his face. The vicar shook his head.

"I'm not sure it can wait," he said. "Perhaps I should go to the police."

"Is something wrong?" Ellie said, her voice suddenly full of concern. "No one has been hurt have they?"

The vicar held out his stubby hands and turned down his mouth. "I really don't know, I pray that no one has."

"What is it?" Georgie said.

The vicar sighed deeply. "Mrs Turnbull came by the parish office just this last hour. I was busy putting together a little proposal around the church vestments fund that I thought Lord Melmersby… anyway, that doesn't matter right now. Mrs Turnbull was terribly upset. It appears her Jim has gone missing."

"Missing?" Ellie and Georgie asked in unison.

"Yes, went out last night and hasn't returned, apparently. Taken his shotgun too. Well, with all his… troubles, of course she's worried that perhaps he's done something unfortunate. Really, it doesn't bear thinking about. I wanted to trouble Lord Melmersby to search the grounds here, the woods and so on. Just in case."

"He might have simply stayed out hunting?" Georgie said, not too convincingly. "Did his mother say he seemed upset?"

"Well, that's the troubling thing," Rev Barton said. "Apparently he was in a terrific state of agitation, she said. Particularly after getting the letter yesterday."

"What letter?"

"Well, it wasn't a letter so much," the vicar said. "Just an envelope with–"

"With a feather in it," Ellie said firmly.

"Why yes," the vicar stammered. "How on earth did you know?"

"Of course!" Ellie said suddenly. "The mouse!"

"Mouse?" Georgie said, studying her friend closely. "Are you quite alright?"

"Is Malkie's car repaired yet?" Ellie said.

"It came back from the mechanics yesterday," Georgie said shaking her head. "Why do…"

"We need to stop Richard before he gets back to Melmersby," Ellie said, grabbing her worn leather car jacket from the coat rack beside the door. "It's a matter of life or death!"

***

"Now I need you to answer two questions, Ellie, before we get wherever you are taking us," Georgie spluttered, gripping her seat edges firmly as the car swung sharply backwards out of the garage, missing the door frame by inches. "Firstly, how the devil did you start this car without the key? And secondly, what on earth does a mouse have to do with any of this?"

"It was Mr Madison, you see," Ellie said, putting her foot hard down on the accelerator to throw up a spray of gravel and power the car out onto the wide drive, sending small stones scattering and rat-a-tatting against the walls of the garage outhouses.

"Mr Madison?" Georgie said incredulously. "The mad feather killer is Mrs Madison's cat? Now I know you have gone completely bonkers!"

Ellie gave a passing glance to the empty roadway then swung the car sharply right out of the entrance gate to Melmersby Hall, throwing Georgie suddenly against the passenger door.

"Steady on, old girl!" Georgie said. "Wherever we are going I'd like to get there in one piece."

"It's not what it seems, you see," Ellie said, looking up for a mirror that wasn't there.

"What isn't?"

"The killer has really been playing cat-and-mouse. They couldn't just go in for the kill straight away, they would never have got away with it. So they've nibbled around the edges, softened up their prey. And now they're about to finish the job off. Looks like we have plenty of time. When did you say Richard was due back?" Ellie rapped her knuckles against the glass of a round-faced clock that protruded from the dashboard.

"About 4:45, I should think," Georgie said. "But that clock is slow. I don't think Malkie had the chance to put it forward last Sunday before he copped it."

"Forward?" Ellie said, looking at Georgie who nervously urged her eyes back on the road.

"Yes, just watch where you are going! I keep forgetting too, and it's a dreadful job with all the clocks and what not at home. The boffins in Whitehall came up with this quite barmy idea to put the clocks forward an hour once a year, heaven knows why. It's all still very new and I've not got used to it yet. So we're running a little late, but that doesn't mean you need to go any faster – we're not going to save anyone if we end up in a ditch!"

Ellie caught a glimpse of Mrs Garnet's face, peeking out from behind the gingham curtains of the tea shop as she sped past. A couple of the cows on the village green turned their faces as well to the noise of the speeding engine roaring through the normally quiet street. Ellie pulled hard on the handbrake to spin the back wheels out and hurl the car around the bend at the end of the village high street, then floored the accelerator to fly over the humped back of the stone bridge that spanned the narrow Melmersby Beck.

"I'm not sure we were fast enough," she said, suddenly sombre, as she stepped hard on the brakes to bring the car to a screeching halt just before the duck pond and the hairpin bend.

Georgie picked herself up from where she'd been thrown forward by the force of the sudden stop. "Ellie! What the devil are you... good Lord! Is that Richard's car?"

Ahead of them, half-mounted on the grass verge of the road, was the black Charron-Laycock that Ellie and Georgie had taken to Scarborough, its front driver's-side tyre blown out and the wing peppered like a colander with small holes. Sat in the driver's seat, Richard had his hands on top of his head, and high up on the bank Jim Turnbull stood, shaking hands gripping the barrel of a shotgun.

"S...stay back please l...ladies. This is between m...me and his lordship," Jim stammered, jabbing the barrel in the direction of the car.

"So that's what he was doing in the road here," Georgie said quietly. "Scoping out an ambush. But Jim? I can't believe..."

"You don't have to do this, Jim!" Richard called out.

"Just you be quiet now, your lordship!" Jim shouted back, his voice shaking nervously. "I know what you done."

"What did I do, Jim?" Richard said, now turning to swing his legs out of the car. "Be a decent fellow like I know you are and at least let me know why you are going to shoot me."

"You get back in that car, sir, or I swear..."

"Jim, don't do it! This isn't the way!" Ellie moved forward to step up the bank and Jim swung the gun down to point at her, then suddenly back at Richard as he now stepped out of the car, his arms raised.

"Get back, both of you!" Jim cried. "I'll do it, I swear."

"Jim–" Richard started.

"You deserved it!" Jim spat, tears now running down his thin cheeks. "You deserved it. You left

Bertie to die, you could have helped him, and you left your own brother. You deserved that feather!"

"Perhaps I did," Richard said solemnly. "Not a day goes by when I don't regret that I didn't do more for him that day. But he wouldn't want this, you know that."

"He was hurt and you left him, I saw it with my own eyes!" Jim shouted back. "You left your own brother."

Richard shook his head. "I wanted to stay with him, and if it was down to me I would have done, and it would have been the wrong thing to do. He knew, and so did I – even if I didn't want to admit it – that there was nothing I could do for him. He ordered me to leave and tend the others, and he was right to do so. So go on, pull the trigger if you want, Jim. Make yourself a killer over something that couldn't have been changed. Do you think that's what Bertie would have wanted for you?"

Jim shook his head. "I don't... don't you play games with me, sir. I loved Bertie, like a brother sir, and he should never have died."

Richard put his hands down and moved slowly towards Jim. "He was my brother, Jim, and goddammit yes, he should never have died. And if I thought for one second that taking my life would bring him back, I would pull that damn trigger myself!"

Jim was shaking violently now, Ellie moved again towards him but Richard put out a firm hand to stop her.

"What about them others, sir? Malkie, Miss Vivienne, Dr Waterman? You killed 'em, and I was gonna be next. You was comin' for me, I know it."

A cough came up from the footwell of the beached car and all heads turned towards it as a familiar head slowly bobbed up from below the back seat.

"I believe reports of my death may have been somewhat exaggerated," a voice said sheepishly.

"Dr Waterman!" Georgie spluttered. "What in blazes...?"

"Richard didn't kill anyone," Ellie said, ignoring Lord Melmersby's firm hand and Georgie's gaping at the seemingly resurrected doctor. She walked slowly up the slope towards Jim. "I believe he's telling the truth. He tried to help his brother but he couldn't, and now he wants to help you, and this time I think he can. He knows you loved his brother, and he knows you didn't mean any of this."

"Get back, miss," Jim said, frantically turning his gun towards Ellie. "Get back or I swear I will shoot, don't think I won't."

Ellie smiled softly, putting out her hand. "You won't, Jim. Because that's not who you are, and because you know Bertie loved us both. Give me the gun. Please?"

Jim swung the gun barrel level to Ellie's head, but she didn't move; her hand still out in front of her, waiting. Jim's jaw tensed, eyes wet with tears and his nostrils flaring, and he let the shotgun fall from his trembling hands, down into the long grass, and stepped forward into Ellie's embrace. She held his stooped back in her arms as it rose and fell to the sound of heavy sobs.

"It's all going to be alright, Jim," Ellie said soothingly. "Richard will make sure you get all the help you need."

"Am I gonna be in trouble, miss?" Jim said, his words punctuated with deep sniffs.

"Not at all, Jim," Richard said, stepping up to where Ellie stood on the bank and putting his hand to Jim's back reassuringly. "Nothing happened here, a bit of glass in the road and a blown tyre that's all. You've been working too hard, old chap – I shall see you get a long convalescent break and some friends of mine will take good care of you."

Richard silently mouthed "thank you" to Ellie, and she smiled back, stepping out of Jim's embrace to let the two doctors help Jim down onto the tarmac of the road.

Georgie stood silently as Ellie walked back towards her, shaking her head and raising her pencilled eyebrows. "Well, I have to say life has certainly not been dull since you got here but that just about tops the lot. Well done you! But if Jim isn't a killer someone still is. What the blazes happens now?"

"Now," Ellie said firmly, stepping back into the driver's seat of the Sunbeam. "Now we go back to Melmersby Hall and have a word with the real killer."

ELLIE BLAINE 1920s MYSTERIES

CHAPTER 22

RICHARD and Dr Waterman loosened their belts to fashion a make-shift tow rope so the damaged car could be pulled back to Melmersby Hall, by way of Jim's mother's house, before too many questions could be asked about how she came to be peppered with holes.

In the other car with Ellie, Georgie had more than a few questions of her own.

"Sorry, so it wasn't Jim; or Richard, obviously. Do you actually know who the feather killer is?"

"I have an idea," Ellie said. "But I need to be sure."

Georgie gave Ellie a wide-eyed stare, prompting her for more, then sighed as Ellie shook her head in response. "Ugh, I see you've taken this detective thing to its logical conclusion. I suppose you'll want everyone in the room when you do your 'big reveal'? Come on, give your old pal a heads-up!"

Ellie laughed half-heartedly. "I've already dropped myself in it once by more-or-less accusing Richard, I think I shall check a few things before I point the finger again."

Georgie let out a grunt of disgust and folded her arms, rapidly unfolding them again to grip the dashboard as Ellie turned more sharply than Georgie would have liked into the grounds of Melmersby Hall. As they pulled up to the wide gravel entrance driveway, they could see the black sedan of DI Lochner parked to the side of the west wing.

"Ah, the real detectives are here,' Georgie said, stressing the word with just enough friendly spite to make Ellie smile. "Perhaps they'll tell me what's going on."

DI Lochner, it seemed, knew no more than Georgie. The sight of Dr Waterman, grinning apologetically as he stepped into the hall, left the detective speechless for a second before he gathered his words and fumbled his notebook out of his pocket.

"Dr Waterman? I thought… where the devil have you been?"

"He's been with me," Richard said. "We thought it best to keep him out of harm's way while there was a killer on the loose, but he called last night and insisted on my bringing him back." Richard glared at his friend accusingly. "I was going to smuggle him into one of the unused rooms, but – well let's just say circumstances have changed."

"I was staying in a little B&B in York," the doctor said, putting his hand to the small of his back and stretching it out. "Old Dickie was kind enough to arrange it all for me and drive me down there, but, well, the bed there was even lumpier than the floor of your car, Dickie."

Richard gave Dr Waterman a look that Ellie suspected carried the message that he was not to call him 'Old Dickie' again anytime soon. Dr Waterman flushed slightly.

"You needed to stay somewhere you wouldn't be recognised, Simon," Richard said sternly. "The next time someone tries to kill you I shall be sure to put you up in the Ambassador Suite at the Crown Hotel, shall I?"

Dr Waterman shrugged apologetically.

"I see," DI Lochner said, nodding to PC Wade to pass him a pencil so he could start jotting things down. "And did you think to mention this to your lady wife, sir?"

Dr Waterman reddened more deeply. "Oh, yes, poor Dotty. I must call her at once. We had to make it seem genuine, you see, to throw the killer off the trail. May I use your telephone Dic... Richard?"

Richard nodded, and Dr Waterman slid, a little awkwardly, out of the hall and into the foyer where the house telephone was kept.

"I'm sorry to interrupt!" Rev Barton had been nursing a pot of tea and a plate of biscuits, his bald head hidden from view by the back of the wingback chair he had nestled into. Opposite him, Archie sat scanning the room and lighting a new cigarette before the old one had fully burned down. The vicar stood up now to address the new arrivals.

"What is it, vicar?" Richard said.

Rev Barton wiped the crumbs of a freshly-dunked Rich Tea biscuit from his upper lip. "I don't suppose you've heard from Jim, have you? I called the officers here, you see, as he's—"

"Jim's fine," Richard said. "We've just dropped him off back at his mother's. He was a little... confused. I shall see that he gets some support. I've taken this off him, just to be safe at the moment." Richard pulled out Jim's shotgun from under his long coat and set it down on the side table in front of the large hall mirror. DI Lochner stared at the weapon intently.

"Oh," Rev Barton said. "Well that is wonderful news. I was so worried. His poor mother was beside herself. I shall be on my way then. DI Lochner, thank you for—"

"If you wouldn't mind, sir, I would prefer everyone to remain here until I have asked a few more questions," DI Lochner said, before turning to face Richard, giving him one of his best interrogation stares. "You say you were keeping Dr Waterman safe from the killer. Yet, it would seem our killer is still out there, unless you know better?"

"Oh! Ellie knows who the killer is, don't you Ellie?" Georgie blurted out, and immediately all eyes turned to Ellie. She wasn't sure if Georgie had just got caught up in the moment, or if this was her mischievous revenge for not being the first to know; but she was absolutely sure that she wished she hadn't said it.

"Gee, thanks Georgie," she said, "nothing like dropping someone in it!" By the way Georgie's face fell, Ellie assumed it hadn't been deliberate.

"Miss Blaine?" DI Lochner said, now turning his stare on Ellie. "Do you have any information pertinent to the recent deaths of Mr Malcolm Fawthrop and Mrs Vivienne Beauclère?"

Ellie saw Archie's head bob up at the mention of his late wife's name, and he drew deeply on his cigarette.

"I'm not sure," Ellie said. "Maybe."

"Maybe?" Richard glared at her now. "Is there something you need to tell us, Miss Blaine?"

Ellie had assumed, after saving Richard's life, that they might be past the 'Miss Blaine' stage, but perhaps that was the name people used when they wanted to make sure she knew they were being serious, she thought.

Dr Waterman stepped back into the room, still grinning nervously. "Phone's on the blink, Richard," he said. "I shan't stay long, I should go and see her really."

"Dr Waterman," Ellie said, turning to Richard's friend who jabbed himself in his chest with his finger as if needing to confirm that she really meant to speak to him at this point. "Would you mind going up to Richard's study and fetching something for me."

"Me?" he said, looking suddenly at Richard for approval and getting a nod. "Well, yes, of course. What is it you want?"

"There's a cabinet in there," Ellie said. "It has a broken latch. There's some papers in there."

"Those are just the estate records," Richard said curiously. "There's nothing terribly exciting in there, I can assure you."

"If you could bring down any records from 1896 and 1897, that would be just dandy," Ellie said, ignoring Richard's protestations.

"Absolutely," Dr Waterman said, his hand shooting up into a sprightly salute as he turned towards the stairs, "I am on it!"

"I'm not sure what you are expecting to find," Richard said. "Whatever it is, I suspect you might be rather disappointed, it's nothing but lists and ledgers."

Ellie looked down, suddenly aware of a movement against her ankles. Mr Madison was rubbing his broad, ginger cheek against her shoe and purring loudly. At the same moment, the door to the kitchen block opened and Mrs Madison strode in.

"Where is that naughty boy! Come here Mr Madison, don't you go disturbing... oh my! Dr Waterman, you're alive!"

Dr Waterman grinned apologetically again and went to speak, before Richard cut in ahead of him. "It's a long story, Mrs Madison, I shall tell you all about it anon. In the meantime, could you bring through some more tea and a few light refreshments? I feel we may be a while here."

Mrs Madison looked back and forth between the two doctors, before shaking the confusion out of her head and wiping her hands on her apron. "Of course, your lordship. Lucy is just back, I shall get her to bring something through for you as quickly as can be." She scooped Mr Madison up with one arm, his long legs dangling inelegantly either side of her thick forearm, and opened the sash window to scoot him out into the garden. "You keep to your rightful place," she called after him as he glared back at her, before turning around to give an indignant shake of his tail in reply.

"Thank you, Mrs Madison," Richard said, before turning back to Ellie. "So what is it exactly you are hoping to find?"

"Just a hunch," she said. "Do you know, I could really do with a scotch right now, anyone else?"

She looked around the room as heads shook at the offer, turning round to the sofa. "Rev Barton? Archie? You'll have one with me, right?"

"What," Archie mumbled. "A scotch? Yes, absolutely, old girl, can't let a lady drink alone!"

Ellie smiled and pulled the stopper on the crystal decanter, half-filling two wide tumblers as Richard scowled. "Here you go," she said, stepping around the bemused vicar to put Archie's glass down on the table, smiling sweetly at him.

"Bottoms up, hey!" Archie said, raising the glass.

"Bottoms up!" Ellie chirped back. "Actually, do you know what? I think a cigarette would go nicely with this."

"A cigarette?" Georgie said, folding her arms tightly. "I didn't know you smoked?"

Ellie had already taken the cigarette Archie had been only too keen to pass her and popped it into her mouth. "It's been a very stressful day," she said. "Sorry Archie, do you have a light?"

Archie was carefully scanning the table, his brow furrowed. "Dash it, my lighter was just here. Where the devil did I put it. Hold this would you, old girl." He handed her his whisky glass while he fumbled in his jacket pocket for his book of matches, pulling one out from it with a sharp tug to spark up a match and light Ellie's cigarette. She gave him a nod of thanks, then drew softly on it, coughing slightly as she did.

"Are you alright, Archie?" She said, "your hand is shaking a little."

"Is it?" he said, glancing at the offending hand. "Well, I jolly well needed that whisky then didn't I!"

"You know," Ellie said. "I think I probably didn't need this cigarette after all, sorry Archie." She stubbed the cigarette out firmly in the glass ashtray on the table, already half full of Archie's burned down stubs.

Dr Waterman had now stepped down the stairs, a bundle of tightly bound papers cradled in his arms. "I think I got them all," he said, placing the documents down on the wide walnut-topped table that filled one corner of the main hall.

"I was thinking," Ellie said, wiping her hands on the hem of her trousers, "when I was looking in your study…" She paused a moment, catching the expression on Richard's face and hoping the heat she felt in her cheeks wasn't showing on her face. "I was wondering why someone would pretend to steal a cup and a pen, and what it was they were really after, and then I thought; what if they weren't after anything?"

"I'm sorry," DI Lochner said. "You're saying whoever broke into Lord Melmersby's study wasn't trying to steal anything? Then why on earth did they break in?"

Ellie flipped quickly through the pile of papers on the table, her hand stopping at a large manila-paper envelope. She picked it up and turned it to show Dr Waterman. "Now this one looks interesting, it has a name and address on it," she said. "Do you recognise it?"

Dr Waterman took the envelope from her and squinted at the spidery blue-black lettering on the front. "Good Lord!" he said suddenly. "Yes I jolly well do. That's addressed to my father!"

"Open it, man!" Richard commanded. "What the devil is this, Miss Blaine? Can you kindly explain yourself?"

Ellie looked around the room. "You see, I don't think the burglar was taking something, I think he was putting something in place. Something that was taken from your surgery, Dr Waterman, when it was broken into a few months ago."

"It's a letter," Dr Waterman said. "It's from Lord Melmersby to my father, it's…"

"Yes?" DI Lochner said. "Could you read it for us, sir?"

Dr Waterman stood open-mouthed for a second. "Um, why, yes. Yes, of course. Let me see: 'Matters pertaining to… January 1897… attending to the death of…' oh, I say!"

"Give it me," Richard said firmly, taking the letter from his friend's hand and scanning it quickly, his heavy brow darkening further with each line.

"What is it, Richard?" Georgie said, tilting her head to try to read across his shoulder.

Richard handed the paper to DI Lochner, his expression unreadable for the moment.

"It seems," Richard said coldly. "That my father was more dishonest than even I gave him credit for."

"Richard?" Georgie said, her voice tinged with concern.

DI Lochner shook his head as he turned the paper over. "It would appear," he said solemnly. "That the late Lord Melmersby had some secrets."

"The letter appears to be by way of settlement on matters relating to the death of a Sarah Elmet," Richard said. "A one-time chambermaid in this house. And it appears she died giving birth to a child. My father's child."

"So that's what Malkie was doing!" Georgie gasped. "That was the secret he kept."

"The child was Lucy," Ellie said.

The men of the room looked suddenly about in bewilderment as Ellie and Georgie nodded to each other. Archie stood up suddenly, dropping his cigarette.

"That's why the late Lord Melmersby was so against Lucy and Bertie's closeness," Ellie said. "And why Bertie so suddenly changed towards her after his talk with Dr Waterman's father."

"And why Lucy got over it so quickly – Bertie would have told her he was her brother!" Georgie said excitedly.

"Exactly!" Ellie said.

"But why would someone want us to know this now?" Richard said. "Why put this in my father's files now?"

"That's the thing," Ellie said. "I don't think we were meant to find it now. I think it was meant to be found after Jim had killed you."

"After Jim what!?" DI Lochner and Rev Barton blurted out the words in unison.

"I'll explain in a bit," Ellie said. The men looked confused. "Richard is the mouse, you see."

"The mouse," Georgie confirmed with a nod. The men looked even more confused.

"The mouse," Ellie repeated. "The murderer couldn't just go straight for the kill, that would be too obvious, too risky, they would be a suspect as soon as this letter was found. They needed to make Richard's death less dangerous to them. There needed to be a motive, he needed to be framed as the killer, and then Jim needed to be convinced he was going to be next."

"The feathers," Richard said. "Of course. Whoever did this must have known about the feathers, known who sent them. Known how it would affect poor Jim, how jumpy he was."

"And known that they would unexpectedly inherit the estate, once you were dead and the last witness had been hanged for your murder. And at that point, Lucy would have made sure someone found the letter."

"Lucy?" Richard spluttered. "You can't be serious?"

"She knew about the feathers," Ellie said. "She told us she saw Malkie, Vivienne and Dr Waterman give them to you. She must have wanted to make sure everyone understood why Jim killed you."

"But what did it have to do with Jim?" Dr Waterman said. "He was nothing to do with our silly nonsense."

"Where did you say you found Jim's letter?" Ellie said.

Richard was lost in deep thought, and took a moment to reply. "Um, I recall it was left under my pillow."

"Is it usual for a gamekeeper to be in your bedroom?" Ellie asked.

"No, I… I suppose it is usual for a chambermaid though?"

Ellie nodded. "Lucy was good friends with Jim, she will have done that job for him I'm sure."

"You're right," Richard said firmly. "And I can be sure you are, or else Malkie would still be alive."

DI Lochner squinted at Richard. "How do you mean, sir?"

"If Lucy saw Malkie give me the feather, that explains why he died. Because if I was the killer, he wouldn't have been touched. That feather was never from Malkie, the poor chap was simply made to do what someone else was too ashamed to do themselves."

"Who was it from then?" Ellie said.

Richard held her gaze for a moment before speaking, and she heard no emotion in his voice. "It was from my mother."

DI Lochner nodded to PC Wade and the two men started towards the door to the kitchen block. Archie suddenly stepped out, raising an admonishing finger in their direction.

"Now hold on!" he said. "Nobody wants to find my wife's killer more than I, but this really does not wash! I can't imagine little Lucy as a killer, nor can you, I'm sure. And besides, she was far from here when my dear Vivienne was taken, and you – yes you, Ellie – you said yourself that she was with you in your room when poor Malkie had his accident."

Ellie nodded. "Yes, but you see that's how I worked out it was Lucy. I thought she was in my room at about 7 o'clock, but I hadn't known to put my watch forward. She must have realised that when I told her the time, she would have thought she'd been given an instant alibi, and that's why she asked to see my watch – so she could change it to the correct time without me realising. She would have thought I'd never know that it was really 8, and that she had had plenty of time to kill Malkie before getting to me. That's why Jim said he saw all the blinds were still shut at 7:30, when, according to my watch, Lucy had already opened mine by then."

Archie shook his head vigorously. "But you said whoever did this must have known the workings of an automobile. How on earth–?"

"Lucy followed Bertie everywhere, she told me that herself," Ellie said. "I assume she spent hours with him in the garage when he was tinkering – long enough to pick up the information she needed to get Malkie under his car."

DI Lochner stepped around Archie. "I've heard enough. PC Wade, would you be so good as to bring Miss Lucy here."

'Wait!" Archie said. "You still can't explain how she could have killed Vivienne if she wasn't here when she died?"

"Oh," Ellie said calmly. "She didn't kill Vivienne. You did."

DI Lochner and PC Wade turned suddenly back to look at Archie, whose face had gone as white as the starched collar he wore on his blue pinstripe shirt. "Me? You can't be serious?"

"You'd no longer need your wife's money, would you," Ellie said, "when you were married to the heir to Melmersby Hall. I imagine that was the arrangement?"

"What in the name of all that is decent are you talking about?" Archie said. "This is preposterous!"

"Thank you for the light, Archie." Ellie said, pulling Archie's lighter from her pocket and holding it up for him to see. "Nice book of matches, you have. You see, when I first saw it I thought it must have been your family crest on it, but Richard put me right and I just wanted to see it again to confirm."

"Me?" Richard said incredulously.

"Yes, just now. The Crown Hotel, York. That's what the matchbook said right? I imagine that is where you went on the 'business trips' Vivienne mentioned. I know it's where Lucy stayed last month when she was in York. I'd even go as far as to say I imagine it was in the same room."

"Now hold on a minute," Archie said, scanning the darkening faces around the room and laughing nervously. "First of all, and may I say, that is outright slander. I… I shall sue! Just you wait. And you can't prove anything. I was alone when I stayed there. Is there a law against staying in a nice hotel?"

"No," Ellie said. "But it seems you are a well-known man in these parts, and Lucy has the sort of face a gentleman doesn't forget easily. It would be simple enough for these officers to put a call in to the hotel and check with the concierge."

Archie's face had now almost turned the same pale blue as his shirt. "I...I."

"Would you like me to make a call, sir?" PC Wade said.

"No!" Archie shouted. "No. You can't. I... It wasn't me. It was Lucy. It was all her idea. I told her not to hurt Vivienne but she said—"

The room shook to a tremendous crack, sending everyone ducking as Archie suddenly flew backwards over the headrest of the armchair. All heads spun back to the table by the mirror, and to Lucy, who stood there with the barrel of Jim's gun breathing blue smoke.

"Very clever, Miss Blaine," she said, a sly grin on her face. "I did worry I took a risk with changing your watch, but I figured you for a dumb blonde American. You're smarter than I thought."

"Lucy, it doesn't have to be like this," Richard said, edging closer toward her. She raised the gun.

"I'm not Jim," Lucy said coldly. "I'm not such a soft-headed coward that I won't pull this trigger. You damn well know I will. And yes, it does have to be like this. It has always had to be like this!"

"You killed people, Lucy," Richard said. "People you grew up with. For what – money? Was it really worth all that?"

Lucy let out a harsh laugh. "Money? You think that's what this is about? Poor silly Richard. Poor little Dickie who so desperately wanted mummy and daddy to love him as much as they loved Bertie. How hard-done-by you were."

"I—" Richard started.

"You have no idea, your lordship," she spat the words. "No idea at all. My mother didn't just die, she was killed. By your father! She gave birth to me in a cold, damp hovel, no heating, no doctor, no midwife, just her, on her own, hidden from the world, while my father had enough money to have bought her silk sheets in a Harley Street clinic."

Richard shook his head sadly. "I am so sorry Lucy…"

"Sorry?" she sneered, "You don't know the half of it. When I found out, when Bertie told me, I was shocked, of course I was. But I was excited too. I had never had a father and I so desperately wanted one. So do you know what I did? Do you know what poor, stupid, naive little Lucy did? I went to your father and I told him I forgave him, that I didn't have to be a secret anymore, that I loved him. I called him daddy!" Lucy's chest was heaving as she spoke. Richard inched closer and she raised the gun again, forcing him to raise his hands.

"I called him daddy. And you know what he called me? He called me a mistake!" Lucy screamed the words, and Ellie instinctively braced for the sound of a gun. Instead, Lucy's voice dropped down to a tone of bitter calm.

"He said if I spoke of it again he would throw me on the street with no reference, and tell people I had stolen from him. So, instead of having a father, I spent the next few years watching the man I knew had rejected me give all his love and attention to the children he wasn't ashamed of, while I waited on them and kept my inconvenient little mouth shut. Yes, even you Richard – you think he didn't love you, but by God I can tell you that if that man had hated you the way he hated me you would have felt it every bit as harshly as I did, and you would know what it is to have your heart broken! This was never about money, I didn't want anything as vulgar as money – I wanted everything, everything that had been denied to me!"

Richard put his hands down slowly, nodding as he did. "Lucy, look – if these facts are known, if it's understood what drove you to this, perhaps we can see some deal done whereby you don't have to hang. I could speak for you–"

Lucy laughed again. "Oh, I have no intention of hanging, or going to prison."

Ellie suddenly looked around the people in the room. "Where's Mrs Madison?" she said in a tone of alarm.

"Oh don't worry," Lucy said. "She's just having a long nap – I gave her a little of what I slipped in your water the first night you were here, to make sure you weren't awake to look out of the window while I was seeing to Malkie. She's the only one here who cared about me, I wouldn't hurt her. But don't mistake that for softness, Lord Melmersby shook that out of me years ago. If only silly little Archie had known me better," she nodded to Archie's lifeless form crumpled across the sofa seat, "he was going to end up like that one way or the other, I just rather wish he'd waited his proper turn."

"Miss Madison, I strongly suggest–" DI Lochner started.

"And I strongly suggest you shut up!" Lucy called back. "I'm not going to prison or the rope. What I'm going to do is walk out of this house, step into that fancy car of Malkie's, and be away and gone before any of you can do anything about it. I've already taken care of the other cars, and the telephone. The gun is a bonus, so thanks for that. I only have one shell, otherwise I'd see the lot of you off, but if you think of following me, I can promise you at least one of you won't live to tell the tale."

Lucy jabbed the barrel in the direction of the huddle to confirm her intent, then backed slowly towards the door, feeling behind her for the handle.

"Lucy–" Ellie started.

"Don't try to stop me, I swear you will regret it," Lucy said, opening the door slowly behind her.

"I'm not going to," Ellie said. "I lost a parent too. I know how much that can hurt. I understand. You deserve another chance."

Richard glared at Ellie and Georgia stared at her, open-mouthed.

"If you are taking the Sunbeam," Ellie said, "you'll need the keys, and I've got them – I'll throw them to you."

Lucy glared suspiciously at Ellie who kept one hand raised and reached carefully into her jacket pocket with the other.

"I learned enough from Bertie that I can start the car perfectly well without them," Lucy snapped, swinging the gun to point at Ellie. "Don't try anything funny."

"It's just the keys, I promise. Might as well make it easier for yourself," Ellie said, "Here, I'll show you." She lifted her hand slowly to reveal the leather pouch key holder, then flicked her wrist to give them a shake and sound out a bright jingle.

"Ok. Give them to me," Lucy called.

"Of course," Ellie said, and gently threw the keys towards Lucy who stepped back to catch them in her free hand, back onto the stone threshold that led onto the driveway, and backwards into the path of a thundering ball of orange fur as it sprinted up the front door steps to the jingling sound of dinner.

Lucy's feet caught up in the scurrying cat and she stumbled backwards, her gun arm lurching upwards in surprise at the sudden impact. A flash of fire and smoke, and the whole room dropped to their knees as the shotgun roared out its hot volley. As the smoke cleared, Lucy lay sprawled out on the hard steps of the doorway, her empty gun flung behind her by the recoil. Before she could scramble to her feet again, PC Wade and DI Lochner sprang up to take her arms, her head dropping in resignation at the fate she knew awaited her now.

Ellie turned round, relieved to see her friends unharmed. Georgie was dusting down her plus-fours with the back of her hands, while Richard rubbed his reddening eyes and shook his head to clear his ears of the ringing. Behind him, high on the wall, Ellie could see what was left of the gold-framed portrait of Lord Melmersby, his forbidding scowl forever wiped clean by the blast of his daughter's gun.

ELLIE BLAINE 1920s MYSTERIES

CHAPTER 23

"DO you suppose she'll hang?" Ellie asked, the tinge of regret in her voice.

The mood was sombre as she and Georgie picked over the remains of their carrot cake in Mrs Garnet's cafe. At least, Ellie thought, the village gossip would have something serious to talk about now.

"I suppose if she hadn't got Archie involved, she might have been able to claim the murders were the act of a desperate mind. But helping a man murder his wife, then shooting the fellow dead? I'm not sure she'll get away with that one."

Ellie nodded, then pushed away the last of her cake, her appetite not up to it right at that moment. "Archie was a bit of a fool, I suppose," she said.

"Poor guy. I really only had a hunch about him, not much evidence – if he'd kept his mouth shut–"

"Poor guy?" Georgie said, leaning over to scoop the remains of buttercream from Ellie's plate. "Did you miss the part about him murdering his wife?"

Ellie shrugged. "I guess you're right."

"So how did you connect the two anyway?" Georgie said.

"Well," Ellie said, "like I say, it was just a hunch. First of all, I realised that whoever took the pen and cup from the study, it wasn't Lucy as she was with Mrs Madison at that time. And whoever it was would have had a car."

"A car?"

"Yes," Ellie said. "The cup and the pen were thrown in the water by the bridge. Whoever took them obviously had no interest in them and wanted rid of them as soon as possible. If they'd walked towards the village from the Hall they'd have been by the riverside as soon as they left the grounds. But if you are in a car, the bridge is the first place you'd come to before you could throw them in the river."

"Gosh," Georgie said, sipping on the lukewarm remains of her Earl Grey, "you really are quite the detective after all, aren't you?"

Ellie smiled. "I don't know about that, just a hunch really. And then there was the – what did Richard call the Mickey Finn?"

"Chloral hydrate, darling," Georgie said.

"That's the one," Ellie said. "Anyway, Richard said his mother hid it about the house but he'd found most of it. So whoever found the last of it must have been someone who knew the house even better than Richard, well that can only have been Lucy or Mrs Madison. I figured that's why she gave me the plum brandy tea, so Richard wouldn't smell it on my breath the next morning after she knocked me out. And of course Lucy would have needed an accomplice to administer it while she was in Harrogate."

"I see," Georgie said. "So Lucy got Archie involved because she needed an alibi for at least one of the murders?"

"And he needed rid of his wife," Ellie said with a sigh. "And then of course he claimed to have come to the hall by bus, but you'd already told me the buses weren't running that day. I suspect it was him I saw skulking in the bushes the night before, he must have been waiting for Lucy to sneak him into the house."

"Do you suppose he thought she would marry him?"

Ellie let out a cold laugh. "If he did he was as much a fool as we all think he was. He was the only witness, and not one who would hold up very well under pressure, it seems. I'm sure he would have been long gone before the secret letter was found and Lucy declared heir to the Melmersby estate. I suspect if Richard's father did leave a will, Lucy made sure that was disposed of too, so the path would be clear for her to inherit when Richard was killed."

"I could almost admire her for it," Georgie said. "Almost."

"So could I," Ellie said. "If she hadn't killed innocent people, or brought poor Jim into her plan. She would have told him all about the feathers, I'm sure; made sure he knew exactly what to think about what they meant, made him believe his life was in danger, encouraged him to act."

"How is old Jim?" Georgie said, suddenly looking up to signal to the eavesdropping Mrs Garnet that she might pop out from behind the beaded curtain with some more Earl Grey.

"Richard said he's sending up some doctor from London to go and talk to him. Apparently there's help he can get for his trauma. None better, he says."

"I do hope so," Georgie said. "Poor chap has been through a lot, and this whole episode will have set him back terribly."

Mrs Garnet arrived, fresh teapot in hand, and placed it carefully on the table without saying a word. Georgie nodded her thanks and she slipped quietly back into her place behind the counter to re-stack a pile of saucers she'd already stacked twice while they'd been talking.

"So what is it for you now?" Georgie said. "You must stay with us a little longer!"

Ellie shook her head. "I need to get back. I have a job at home that they'll only keep open for a short while, and only because they knew my father. And my mom will be missing me, not that she'd ever say it. Richard is leaving for London tomorrow and has been kind enough to offer me a lift to York Station. There's a boat leaving Southampton in three days, so I'll have time for a bit of sightseeing down there."

"Oh what a dreadful shame. I shall miss you terribly of course, and you will write every month and naturally you shall come back to visit when I take my place at the Bar."

"You got in?" Ellie said, an excited smile breaking out across her face.

"I did indeed," Georgie said. "All those dreary dinners paid off in the end."

"That's just swell!" Ellie beamed. "Well done!"

"Yes," Georgie said, bowing theatrically. "Swell is exactly what it is. The absolute swellest! Of course, I won't be a barrister yet. That's the next hurdle to jump, but you know what my motto is: 'you win your race one stride at a time!'"

"Well, that's a pretty big stride," Ellie said, raising her teacup in salute. "Here's to you and winning your race."

"Cheers!" Georgie smiled, chinking her cup against Ellie's. "Bottoms up! And here's to you too, Ellie Blaine, Private Investigator! You have been spiffing company."

"You too," Ellie laughed. "The absolute spiffingest."

* * *

Richard had been away from the Hall for the last two days, attending to Jim's care and dealing with the aftermath of the police investigation. He had broken the news to Mrs Fawthrop about the nature of Malkie's death, and she in turn had told him about what she did with Lord Melmersby's bequest to her husband. Ellie had heard, from someone who heard it from someone who heard it from Mrs Garnet, that Richard had asked how much Malkie had been left, and then given her double the amount because he believed her too modest to tell him the real figure.

Ellie wasn't sure why, but that news had brought a lump to her throat. Perhaps at the thought of poor widow Fawthrop, or maybe because she knew it was the sort of thing Bertie would have done. For most of the time she had been at Melmersby Hall she couldn't wait to leave; now she was leaving she thought she might have liked to stay just a little longer.

There had been one change at the Hall since the terrible events just a week before. Poor Mrs Madison had taken Lucy's downfall badly and so she had been given as long as she needed to take a break at her sister's home in Cleethorpes. In the meantime, Richard had employed a new butler, chauffeur and chambermaid to lighten her load when she returned. Ellie couldn't help but feel they might just put the housekeeper's nose out of joint more than they helped, but she would get used to them.

There was still one familiar face here, and Ellie winked at the ginger ball of fur that rubbed his cheek against her travel case as she waited for the chauffeur to turn the car out of the garage, and for Richard to join her.

"Hello Mr Madison," she said softly. "Sorry to see me go?"

Mr Madison let out a high trill and shook his bottle-brush tail.

"I shall miss you too," Ellie said. "We made a good team."

"Ah, there you are!" Richard barked. "Has the new butler not helped you with your case?"

Ellie shook her head. "I told him not to bother," she said. "I've managed my life so far without a butler, and I can manage the rest of it without one too, I'm sure."

"At least let me help you with your bag," Richard said. He picked the bag up, and Ellie felt it would be impolite to do anything now other than nod thanks for his completely unnecessary effort.

"Are you sure you have enough for the journey?" Richard said. "It's rather a long drive. Might you take a little to eat?"

"York's only half an hour away," Ellie said. "Well, maybe a bit longer if I'm not driving, but I'm sure I will manage. Thank you all the same, that's very kind."

Richard glanced quickly at the driver, then back at Ellie. "I was rather wondering if you might make the journey all the way to London with me.

You could get a train from there too, or – well there is something else I wished to discuss with you."

Ellie narrowed her eyes, unsure of where the conversation was going. "Something else?"

"Yes," Richard said. "Well the thing is, you'd need to sign papers and what not, and my lawyers are in London, so–"

"Lawyers?" Ellie said, looking around for someone to explain what was going on, although there was no-one else there but the driver.

"Yes. You see, well, it's a cold place, you see. I mean, not cold as in chilly. Well yes it is, but that's not the point. But to me, it's cold. It's not somewhere I…"

"What are you talking about, Richard?" Ellie said, fixing his gaze to try to bring his mind back to a place where he put his words in the correct order.

"Well, dash it, what I'm trying to say is that it's yours. If you want it."

Ellie held up her hands. "Want what?"

"Melmersby Hall," Richard said. "It's yours if you want it. Of course it's a devil to keep running and certainly not cheap, but the income from the lands just about covers it with a little to spare so–"

"Wait a minute! Wait a minute!" Ellie wasn't sure now if the stress of the last few days had finally separated Richard from his senses, or whether he was simply making some joke at her expense. "You can't give me Melmersby Hall!"

"Well actually I can," Richard said, recomposing himself at last. "I am Lord Melmersby and I can jolly well do whatever I like with it. But that's not the point. It's not me giving you the hall, it's Bertie."

"Bertie?" Ellie said, more confused than ever.

"Yes, Bertie," Richard said. "Jim was right. I did leave my brother's side as he lay dying. There were men to tend, good men, men who still had some hope of surviving. But I came back, before the end. I was with him when he... when he slipped away. He loved you, Miss Blaine, as much as a chap can love a girl. I know that. And he wanted me... he asked me, at the last, to make sure you were taken care of.

"You should know, he only broke the engagement because in his heart he knew he would never make it through the war. He was just too damn brave, too damn selfless, for that. He thought if you had moved on from him, well then you wouldn't be so hurt. That was the only thing that scared him, Ellie: not the guns, not the enemy, not dying; just the thought of hurting you. If that damned war hadn't taken him, I know he would have married you and you would be Lady Melmersby now. So this is the best I can do, to pretend, to make it a little as if everything had gone as it should have done. To give you a part of Bertie, because this was always his home, not mine. He was happy here, and now you should be."

Ellie took a deep breath and she felt something break, something hard and brittle; something that had kept part of her locked away every day since she got that telegram from England all those years ago, and she finally let all her tears flow.

Richard raised a hand, as if to comfort her, then awkwardly drew it back. "It's alright, Miss Blaine. It's just, um. Yes, I suppose one should cry. I shall give you a moment."

"No, wait," Ellie said, sniffing deeply and wiping her eyes with the sleeve of her blouse. "Thank you. Thank you for your offer, and thank you for your words, which mean far more to me than even the grandest house in England could."

"You accept the offer then?" Richard said.

"I'll think about it, on the way to London. There's a lot to consider."

Richard smiled, a little uncertainly. "Jolly good, well we should probably best get going."

"You know, I'm sorry," Ellie said, as she shouldered her small bag.

"Whatever for?" Richard said.

"For thinking you were the murderer."

Richard snorted. "Oh, don't worry, you weren't the only one. We were all victims of a very cunning and capable young woman. She fooled us all. Well, nearly all of us anyway."

Ellie smiled more broadly, wiping away the last of her tears from her cheek. "Bertie always said you were terribly serious and strict but that under it all there was a big softie." she said. "I'm starting to think he was right."

Richard's face flushed a little, just for a second before he brought it back under control. "Did he now? Well he never had anything but gushing praise for you, as I'm sure you can imagine. I thought he was quite mad, of course, to make a match with some…"

"Silly American sales girl?"

"Well," Richard said dryly, "those are your words, not mine, but in a roundabout way… Anyway, what I'm getting at is I suppose I can understand now why he did."

Ellie shook her head. "So you don't think I'm an 'impetuous, hot-headed, over-confident and brash American who doesn't know her place' anymore, then?"

Richard looked her up and down for a second, then flicked his hand dismissively. "Oh, that is exactly what you are," he said, a subtle smile playing on his lips. "It's just that I finally understand now why a chap like Bertie would think that might make you his perfect Lady Melmersby."

Richard opened the car door and Ellie stepped inside. Richard moved around the other side of the car to take his place on the far end of the passenger seat.

"Do you mind if I read my Times?" he said. "It helps the journey go by more quickly."

Ellie nodded. "Be my guest," she said.

The engine kicked into life and the car pulled slowly away to the soft sound of crushed gravel. As they turned onto the drive, Ellie looked back to the yellow stone of Melmersby Hall, to the tulips and roses that broke the ground along the avenue of cherry blossom and willow, and at the dappled light that warmed the deep fresh green of spring. And she thought this was exactly how she had imagined England to look.

A SECRET OF FEATHERS

ELLIE BLAINE 1920s MYSTERIES

A SECRET OF FEATHERS

ELLIE BLAINE 1920s MYSTERIES

1: A Secret of Feathers
2: The Dozen Witches
3: The Cat from Nowhere
4: A Race to the Death
5: A Very Peculiar Piece
6: The Malabar Hotel Mystery
7: A Sliver of Doubt
8: The Purple Gecko
9: A Secret of Hearts

ELLIE BLAINE 1920s MYSTERIES

ABOUT THE AUTHOR

EM Bolton is the pen name of a husband and wife writing team from the English Cotswolds. He's an historical fiction author and award-winning journalist, she helps disadvantaged children to learn through interaction with nature, when she's not plotting diabolical ways to bump off an assortment of historical characters. They are ably assisted by their old – and very high-maintenance – cat, Snowpea.